Cara's Beach Party
Disaster

The
Twelve Candles Club

Cara's Beach Party Disaster

Elaine L. Schulte

BETHANY HOUSE PUBLISHERS
MINNEAPOLIS, MINNESOTA 55438

Published in association with the literary agency of Alive Communications, P.O. Box 49068, Colorado Springs, CO 80949.

Cover illustration by Andrea Jorgenson.

Published by Bethany House Publishers
A Ministry of Bethany Fellowship, Inc.
6820 Auto Club Road, Minneapolis, Minnesota 55438

Printed in the United States of America

Library of Congress Cataloging-in-Publication Data

Schulte, Elaine L.
    Cara's beach party disaster / Elaine Schulte.
        p.   cm. — (The Twelve Candles Club ; bk. 3)
    Summary: Her older half-sister's teasing and cruel pranks cause Cara many problems and bring about the first rift among the members of The Twelve Candles Club.
    [1. Sisters—Fiction. 2. Clubs—Fiction. 3. Christian life—Fiction.]
  I. Title. II. Series: Schulte, Elaine L. Twelve Candles Club ; 3.
PZ7.S3867Car   1993
[Fic]—dc20   92-43515
                                                                        CIP
ISBN 1–55661–252–4   AC

To the real Bear

ELAINE L. SCHULTE is the well-known author of twenty-five novels for women and children. Over a million copies of her popular books have been sold. She received a Distinguished Alumna Award from Purdue University as well as numerous other awards for her work as an author. After living in various places, including several years in Europe, she and her husband make their home in San Diego, California, where she writes full time.

CHAPTER

1

"Slumber party! Slumber party!" the girls chorused from the street outside Cara Hernandez's bedroom window.

Sitting on the edge of her twin bed, Cara half felt like yelling an excited "Slumber party!" herself. The other half of her felt nervous, as if something bad were going to happen. She pulled on her white thongs and rushed for the hallway.

It was a sunny California evening in June, almost too beautiful for anything to go wrong. She'd polished her family's small one-story Spanish-style house to sparkling, and, best of all, her half sister Paige was leaving for the night. This summer was going to be the greatest of her entire twelve years, Cara told herself firmly, and it was because she belonged to the Twelve Candles Club.

"Pizza!" her friends yelled from the street. "Bring on the pizza!"

Smiling at them, Cara darted a glance at herself in the entry

9

mirror: white shorts, white T-shirt, brown eyes shining in her heart-shaped face, and bouncy dark hair. She wasn't cute, pretty, or beautiful, but she looked friendly, maybe even poetic as a writer should.

Her older half sister, Paige Larson, slipped up behind her in the mirror's reflection. "Well, aren't you something, *Caroleen-a* Hernandez? Maybe a Miss Mexico if you'd only move there."

Clenching her fists, Cara tried to ignore Paige's insult. But as she backed away, Paige pressed her pretty face against Cara's to look in the mirror. Her half sister's snug red shorts outfit contrasted with her long, tousled blond hair, and she beamed her cheerleader smile. They had the same mother, but they couldn't be more unalike. Even their smiles were different: Paige's, a snobby look-at-me, and Cara's, a quiet don't-look-too-hard-at-me.

Turning, Paige eyed Cara's outfit. "White shorts and Tee again . . . that's all you wear. Of course, it looks good with your brown skin."

At least I don't have to lie out at the beach all summer to get a tan, Cara thought, not caring to rehash the subject. Besides, Paige lived in red and black clothes.

What was taking her friends so long to get to the door?

She snapped at Paige, "I thought you were leaving."

"Forgot something." Her sister headed into the living room. "Don't worry, I'll leave by the back door so you babies can have your cute little Twelve Candles Club slumber party. By the way, here's a video tape for you."

"What is it?" Cara asked, suspicious.

"Don't worry, it's PG–13. No parental guidance for thirteen-year-olds and up. Or is PG–13 too *old* for you children?"

"Stop it, Paige!" Cara said. She turned, but not before seeing Paige put the tape on the TV cabinet.

"I dare you to show it," Paige said. "I double dare you, *Caro-leen-a* Hernandez!"

Cara clenched her fists. "I am not Carolina except in Spanish, which you refuse to speak! And you don't always have to make Hernandez sound so insulting, either. There are a lot of good things about being part-Hispanic—or even all Hispanic, if I were." She almost added, *at least I have a father,* but that would really be too mean since Paige's father had disappeared when she was a baby. Nobody talked about it.

Finally, her friends rang the doorbell and pounded out a *knock-knock, knock-knock-knock-knock* on the front door. "Order in the court, the monkey wants to speak," they chorused as crazy as ever.

Cara decided not to let Paige spoil her slumber party. "Leave us alone!" she muttered. "Just leave us be!"

"I'm going-going-going before you lose your Latino temper!" Paige answered, flipping her blond hair and starting for the kitchen. "I'm just glad I'm not a stupid-stupid-stupid twelve-year-old."

Paige was the one with the temper, Cara thought. Not her or her father, who was the only total Latino in the family.

She let out her breath, pasted on a smile, and pulled open the door just as her friends began another *knock-knock, knock-knock-knock-knock.*

"Hi!" She felt a little shy, even with them. "Come on in."

They all wore white shorts and Tees, too, as if it were the club uniform.

"Hurray!" Tricia cheered as they trooped in with their sleeping bags and overnight stuff. "Hurray for Club El Wacko, the wackiest club in the West!"

Cara had a feeling that her sister was watching from around the kitchen corner, and for the first time, she saw her Twelve Candles Club friends through Paige's snobbish eyes:

Vice-president, Jess McColl, short and sturdy, built like the gymnast she was, a grin on her no-nonsense face, and plain light brown hair . . . *President,* Becky Hamilton, tall and lanky and a little klutzy, a white headband holding back her long brown hair . . . *Treasurer,* Tricia Bennett, a dramatic blondish redhead with matching thick brows and lively green eyes.

Not one of them was Paige's idea of the "right kind of friend"—the type who'd be wildly popular and a cheerleader. But who knew what they'd look like when they were going on seventeen like Paige?

The back door slammed, and Jess asked, "Paige leaving?"

Cara nodded. "She's staying at a friend's."

"Good news," Jess said. "She's always sneering down her nose at us."

The motor of Paige's red Thunderbird roared as she backed it down the driveway, then squealed the tires as she drove away.

"Whoa! Listen to her go!" Tricia exclaimed. "She'll get a ticket for sure."

"Won't be the first one," Cara answered. In January, Paige had inherited money from her Grandmother Larson. She'd bought the car, redecorated her room with red carpeting, black lacquered furniture, and rock star posters, then bought her red and black look-at-me clothes.

"Dad says she's always testing the limits," Cara said, then drew a breath. "Come on. Let's put your sleeping bags and stuff in my room."

"Y-es!" Becky answered, making it sound like a cheer.

"Yahoo!" Jess yelled to sound crazy.

As they passed the living room TV, Tricia noticed the video tape Paige had left for them. "All right . . . a video for tonight! What a g-r-e-a-t deal for your father to have a video store!"

"Sometimes," Cara admitted. Paige's words flashed through her head again. *"I dare you! I double dare you to show it! Or is PG–13 too old for you?"*

Becky stooped to pull her white sandal back on. "It's great that you can use Flicks' video camera to tape our slumber parties and clown routines and stuff, too."

Cara nodded. "I thought we'd record our klutz act."

She'd no more than mentioned it than they dropped their sleeping bags and went into their usual klutz act: crossed their eyes, turned in their knees, and stumbled about wildly. "Klutz . . . klutz . . . klutz!" they chorused.

"You wackos!" Cara laughed as her white cat streaked from the couch and out the room. "Even Angora's running from you!" She finally quit laughing enough to ask, "You want me to record it now?"

"No way!" Tricia answered. "And have you sell it to a TV station, too?"

Cara grinned. "You know I'd never do that."

Tricia tipped her sleeping bag up on one end and sat down. "Maybe you'll be a writer *and* photographer," she said. "You're good at both. And you know what God says about giving us at least one talent. Maybe you have two or three talents, or even more."

"Maybe," Cara agreed, although Tricia and Becky were the ones who knew what the Bible said, not her. "I wish I had my own camera, so I could always have it with me."

"What about the burglar chase you sold to Channel 10 for

the news?" Becky asked. "Didn't they pay you lots?"

Cara shook her head. "I'd have to sell ten more to buy my own video camera. They don't pay much to amateurs."

"At least it was on TV," Tricia said proudly. "It's a good credit."

Jess eyed Cara. "What did Paige say when she saw your film on TV?"

Cara shrugged. "Nothing. I guess she didn't like it."

"Figures," Jess said.

Tricia bounced with excitement. "Well, I thought it was wonderful! When 'Film by Cara Hernandez' came on the TV news, I thought 'That's our Cara, member of the Twelve Candles Club and one of my best friends.' "

Cara grinned. It was nice to have them as friends—the best she'd ever had.

"You know Paige had to be jealous," Becky told Tricia. "Anyhow, Cara, with all the money we're making in the club, you'll be able to buy your own video camera—a really good one—by the end of this summer."

Cara shook her head as they gathered their gear and trooped down the hallway to her room. "I don't think so." For one thing, her father was spending lots of money to get the family video business going in the bigger cities in Mexico. For another, it cost lots for Mom to be back in college. "I'll use it to buy school clothes and maybe decorate my room a little."

She eyed her bedroom. Compared to Paige's dazzling room, her own looked d-u-l-l. It was almost the same now as when they'd first bought their small three-bedroom house in Santa Rosita Estates years ago: tan carpet, creamy walls, and matching shutters at the windows.

Right after they'd moved in, they'd found the maple furniture at a yard sale, and, last Christmas, her parents had given her the flowery quilted bedspread for her twin bed and a matching cushion for her window seat. The bedspread had peach, yellow and coppery flowers, and last month in Mexico, Dad had bought her matching silk flowers to set on top of the chest of drawers.

Paige called the decor "stupido nothing," but when Cara had waxed the maple furniture to a mellow glow for tonight's slumber party, she'd felt content. In her journal she'd written, *If I'm going to be a writer, I can't live in a room that screams look-at-me, look-at-me! I need quiet.*

Becky, the artist among them, surveyed the room. "How would you redecorate?"

"Just little touches. Maybe a wicker bird cage to hang from the ceiling and put silk flowers in it. And maybe on the wall a big print of flowers."

"Sounds good," Becky decided. "Just like you . . . quiet in a cheerful and thoughtful way."

So that's how Becky saw her, Cara thought. Cheerful and thoughtful—not shy.

"Enough decorating talk," Jess said. She plopped onto the tan carpet, rolled onto her back, and began to bicycle her legs. "What'll we do now?"

Cara shrugged. "Mom and Dad are bringing pizzas when they come home from Flicks after seven."

"Good," Becky said. She straightened her spine like she always did when she remembered she was president of their club. "That gives us time for a fast meeting now, since we skipped meeting at Jess's this afternoon." She sat down backwards on Cara's desk chair, her long legs stretched out in front of her. "This meeting of the Twelve Candles Club will now come to order."

Jess kept on bicycling, but Cara and Tricia had taken out their daily planning calendars and settled with a bounce on the flowery twin bed.

Cara reached for her secretary's notebook from the lineup of books on her desk. Finding the page in her secretary's notebook, she wrote in the date and *Cara's room.*

"Any old business?" Becky asked.

Tricia raised a hand. "We could go over our plans for working the big real estate party tomorrow."

Jess's mom, a realtor, had gotten the job for them; she'd even talked her boss into letting Becky make the party invitations. "It'll be easy," Jess said, still bicycling her legs. "It's an outdoor buffet by the Tuckers' pool, so we'll offer appetizers, put out food, and clean things up. Let's wear our white skirts and blouses—and the white candle necklaces so everyone knows we're hired help."

"Ha! We'll be the only kids there!" Becky said. "The *only* kids. That means, at least, we won't have to baby-sit too."

"Anyhow, the work sounds simple," Tricia remarked, "but on these big jobs, there's always a glitch."

"A what?" Becky asked.

"A glitch. You know, unexpected trouble," Tricia explained. "A burglar swipes the guests' purses or the caterer hates us . . . or . . . maybe that kidnapper they've been talking about on TV comes."

"Is that all!" Becky giggled.

Cara giggled with her, remembering the party at Mrs. Llewellyn's where the first two things had actually happened.

Jess shook her head. "The only thing I can think of that

might go wrong is with Mom's boss, Mr. Tucker. He's a real grouch."

"What does he look like, so we know?" Cara asked.

"Kind of short and potbellied—and he wears a black toupee," Jess replied.

Cara gave a laugh. "A toupee? You mean a wig?"

Jess nodded, grinning. "Only on the top of his head, which is what makes it a toupee."

"We'll have to pray about him," Becky said.

"You mean we should pray for him to *grow hair?*" Tricia laughed. "Maybe grow it right there at the party? Wouldn't that be a sight?"

At the thought of it, they all roared, and Jess finally managed, "His wife is grouchy too."

"We'll pray for her to grow hair, too!" Tricia shrieked, and they all laughed wildly again.

When they'd calmed down, Cara decided not to write anything about the Tuckers, or about praying, in her secretary's notebook. The trouble with being in a club with Christians like Becky and Tricia was that you heard a lot about it, one way or another. Not that there was anything wrong with it.

When Cara looked up, Becky was digging in her overnight bag. "Here's the car-washing list for tomorrow morning." She handed each of them a copy. "Fifteen cars to wash every Saturday morning now. We'll have to work fast to be ready for Mr. Tucker's real estate party at one o'clock."

She turned to Jess, who was still bicycling her legs. "Any other old business like phone calls this afternoon, O Keeper-of-the-Club-Telephone?"

Jess kept on bicycling. "Only two. One baby-sitting cancellation, and switching the Terhunes' Saturday afternoon housecleaning because of the Tuckers' party. It's all taken care of. No problems."

"Thank you, Jess."

"Right on, Jess!" Tricia said.

"Any other old business?" Becky asked. "Oops, almost forgot the treasurer's report."

Tricia opened her treasurer's book. "We have $24.55 . . . enough to buy craft stuff and midmorning snacks for Morning Fun for Kids. We're paid up for the clown outfits and supplies for birthday parties. Any other bills?"

They all shook their heads.

Becky raised a hand. "I was wondering if we should pay part of Jess's phone bill every month since we're using her phone as the call-in number?"

Jess shook her head. "Dad's happy to pay for it. He figures my working in the club saves him lots of money."

"All right! Tell him thanks for us," Becky said. She looked through some notes. "Any new business?"

They all shook their heads again.

"Hurray! I move that this meeting be adjourned!" Tricia declared. "Let's watch the video!"

Cara hesitated, nervous again. "Maybe . . ."

Jess rolled back from bicycling her legs and sprang to her feet. "Maybe what?"

Paige's words returned to Cara's mind: *I dare you! I double dare you.* . . .

"Come on," Cara said, heading for the hallway. "We've worked hard enough all week. We deserve a movie."

The living room was mostly white with tan furniture and carpeting, which made it dull, except for the batik throw pillows and colorful paintings from India that Mom liked—which seemed all wrong for a Spanish-style house.

Cara stuck the video in the VCR while her friends flopped down on the tan carpet.

"What is it?" Tricia asked, excited. She knew a lot about movies and plays because she wanted to be a serious actress. Sometimes she even acted in her church skits and the Christian Community Theater.

"*Moonstreams* or something like that," Cara answered. "The cover wasn't on it." She sat on the floor against the couch with the remote control and turned it on.

The film started with dreamy music and *Moonstreams* was spelled out over a shot of a beautiful moonlit beach. As soon as the opening credits ended, a scantily dressed woman ran across the beach, and people yelled really bad four-letter words as they chased her. When they caught her, the movie got so bad that Cara felt her mouth drop open.

"Turn it off!" Tricia demanded. "Turn that awful thing off. You know Becky and I aren't allowed to see that kind of stuff. It must be R-rated . . . or even worse!"

"You know Flicks sends R-rated movies back to the distributor. It's PG–13." Cara could tell they didn't believe her, so she said it again, "PG–13."

Tricia flung a batik pillow at Cara. "I don't care what it's rated. It's a d-i-r-t-y movie and it will p-o-l-l-u-t-e our perfectly good minds. We're to think about things that are honorable . . . and right and pure and beautiful and . . . and respectful! Watching movies like this is dancing at the devil's doorstep."

"You got that from your minister grandfather!" Cara said, her temper rising.

"You're right about that," Tricia answered. "He knows what's best for us."

Despite the screams on the video, Cara grew more furious by the moment, and she tossed the cushion back. "Dancing on the devil's doorstep?! You're crazy!"

"Stop it," Becky announced in her most presidential tone. "Stop fighting and stop the movie!"

To her own surprise, Cara retorted, "You're not the president of my house!" She grabbed another cushion and threw it at Becky, who looked shocked. "Besides, Paige said this movie is PG–13!"

"Paige?" Tricia asked, getting to her feet. "*Paige* gave it to you?"

Cara nodded, trying to ignore the dirty words coming from the video.

Tricia hesitated, then said in a serious tone, "I don't believe that movie is PG–13, Cara. I just don't believe it. If you don't turn it off, I'll have to go home."

For an instant, Cara wondered if Paige had played a trick on her, not that it'd be at all surprising. But how dare Tricia and Becky tell her what to do in her own house! "I'm not going to turn it off."

"What did you say?" Becky asked, her blue eyes wide. She stood up now, too.

"I'm not going to turn it off," Cara repeated. "If you don't like my house . . . then, well, I guess you'll just have to . . . you'll just have to go home!"

Tricia and Becky eyed each other in amazement, then nodded.

"Okay, if that's what you want," Tricia said unhappily.

They turned and headed toward Cara's room for their sleeping bags and overnight stuff.

Despite everything, Cara couldn't believe they would actually leave. Just minutes ago they'd said they were proud of her video on Channel 10, that she was thoughtful and—

"It's a bad movie, Cara," Jess said. "Not even my brothers would be allowed to watch it."

"Not you, too, Jess! How can you side with them! I thought you were my best friend."

Jess rolled over on her back and started to do stomach crunches, not watching the movie, and Cara's throat tightened so much she could hardly get her breath.

"Jess. . . ?"

Jess didn't answer.

When Tricia and Becky returned with their sleeping bags and stuff, they shot a glance at the movie, which was getting worse and worse.

"We don't want to do this," Tricia began.

"You're the ones who don't like it, so you can just be the ones to get out of here!" Cara retorted. Even as she spoke the words, something in her wanted to apologize, but her anger and stubbornness made her rush on recklessly. "Do you think I care about your stupid club?"

Becky gasped, probably because the idea for the club had been hers.

Tricia shook her head. "Cara, you can't mean this . . . not you—"

"You mean not *shy* little me!" Cara flung back at her. "Well, maybe I'm tired of being pushed around!"

"It's a dirty, ungodly movie!" Tricia returned.

They started out the door, and Becky said, "Jesus wouldn't want us watching this movie, Cara. I can't stay, either."

It wasn't until the door closed behind them that Cara realized what she'd done. Before they'd arrived, she'd been so happy about this slumber party, about the Twelve Candles Club, and about having good friends.

As she clicked off the video, hot tears burst to her eyes. Paige was right about one thing: Cara Hernandez had a temper—Latino or not.

Determined not to cry, it was a long time before she could turn around to face Jess.

CHAPTER

2

*J*ess let out a big breath. "Let's go ride our bikes to cool off. We can still be back in plenty of time for your parents to get here with the pizzas."

Cara glanced at the mantelpiece, where a shiny brass clock with a spinning whirligig stood under a bell-shaped glass. It was just six-thirty. "I don't know what Mom and Dad will say about Tricia and Becky leaving."

Jess shrugged. "Just tell them the truth. Say we had a fight. You don't have to tell what about."

Cara rewound the movie and ejected it from the VCR so her parents wouldn't turn it on accidentally. "I'll . . . I'll just say Tricia and Becky had to go home. That's true anyhow." She felt sure that Jess didn't like being mixed up in this and might leave, too. "Hold on. I'll write a note for Paige and put it with the video in her room."

Jess grabbed the back of the couch and did leg stretches, not answering.

"Hold on," Cara said again, then hurried down the bedroom hallway for Paige's room.

As usual, it was a jolt to walk into the forbidden red, black, and white room. Her half sister's expensive clothes lay in rumpled heaps all over the red carpeting, and her answering machine's red light was blinking. Probably guys phoning for dates or calls from Paige's rich girlfriends.

Cara stepped around the mess and was putting the video on the black lacquered chest of drawers when she saw the video tape box, *Moonstreams*.

The rating was R!

R!

Cara stood staring, then fury rose to her throat. Paige had lied . . . probably hoping she'd make trouble. And it wasn't the first time she'd lied, either.

Madder yet, Cara decided not to leave a note with the video. Why apologize for coming into Paige's oh-so-private room? Why apologize for anything at all? She rushed for the door, tempted to stomp all over her sister's clothes. Instead, she just slammed the door hard.

In the living room, Jess had switched to side stretches. She'd exercise her way through an earthquake, Cara thought, hurrying past. She blurted out, "The rating was R!"

"Coming from Paige, I'm not surprised," Jess answered, still doing side stretches. "You going to tell your parents?"

"I don't know. No, I guess not." They'd be furious with Paige, but it'd probably lead to more of "Dad-is-only-Paige's-stepfather" arguments between him and Mom. And Cara didn't like to hear them fighting. It was scary with so many parents getting divorced.

She told Jess, "Wait till I write a note for my parents so

they don't worry about our being gone."

Jess didn't answer, so Cara hurried to the kitchen.

On the white-tiled counter by the phone, she grabbed a piece of paper and wrote, *Jess and I are going to be out riding our bikes. We'll be back by seven. The others had to go home.*

When she returned to the living room, Jess headed for the front door. "Ready?"

"Ready," Cara answered, relieved to get out. The air in the house seemed so thick with trouble that it choked her. She felt like running to escape.

Outside, the fresh air and the sound of the birds made her feel better. She got her bike from the carport, hopped on and coasted down the driveway alongside Jess, then looked up and down their street. As usual, it was quiet since people didn't hang out in their front yards in Santa Rosita Estates. Best of all, there was no sign of Becky or Tricia. One thing for sure, she didn't want to see them.

They headed across the street toward Jess's house. "My bike's in the garage," Jess said as if they hadn't been neighbors for years.

"Where else?" Cara answered to fill the strange silence between them.

The McColl house was a custom two-story, built on a double lot; it was probably the most expensive house in Santa Rosita Estates. People said it was because Mrs. McColl had gotten a good buy since she'd been the realtor in charge of selling the development—and also because she liked to look richer than her neighbors. Luckily, Jess was not like her mother.

Jess rode her bike out of the garage. "We're off!"

"Way off!" Cara answered, then realized she was trying hard to fill the silence again.

"That's Tricia's line," Jess reminded her.

Cara nodded. "Let's not talk about them. And let's not ride past their houses, either."

They rode south on La Crescenta, which eventually led to a dead end. And *dead end* was exactly how she felt now about the Twelve Candles Club. Probably the club would split up and be ruined forever.

She pedaled hard behind Jess, and, after a while, riding along with the breeze in her hair felt good. Finally, she said, "We'd better not go far and be too late."

Jess stopped pedaling and coasted along. "I have an idea . . . let's get even with Tricia and Becky."

"How?"

"After dark, we can TP—you know, toilet paper—their front yards."

"TP their yards?!" Cara exclaimed. The idea sounded crazy, but before long, it began to seem like a good suggestion. After all, Tricia and Becky had been the ones who'd walked out on her slumber party!

"All right, let's do it." She paused, though. "You don't think it would make things . . . you know . . . worse?"

"Nah," Jess answered. "Everyone does it. Besides, TP-ing someone's yard is just a joke."

"I guess so. But I've never done it."

"No big deal," Jess told her. "I did it with my brothers."

When they pedaled their bikes back into Cara's driveway, the *Flicks Family Videos* white minivan was just pulling in.

"Where are the other girls?" her father asked as he climbed out, his brown eyes shining. His dark beard had grown out a

26

little since this morning, but he looked nice anyhow. People said Arturo Hernandez was the most handsome man in the neighborhood, and Cara believed it. More important, he was a good person.

"I . . . ah . . . left a note for you and Mom inside," Cara answered. "They had to go home."

"At least it won't be so noisy," Mom said, getting out the van's other side. "I have to study again this weekend."

Dad shot a disappointed look at her, but didn't say anything. Sometimes he complained that she cared more about going to college to be a school counselor than she cared about her own daughters. And sometimes Cara was sure of it, which hurt a lot.

As usual, Mom wore a jeans outfit and carried an armful of books. With her wavy dark blond hair and dreamy gray-blue eyes, she looked almost like a college girl. Paige had inherited their mother's upturned nose and oval face, but had her missing father's blonder hair—the father Mom sometimes slipped and called Mad Dog Larson.

Cara's father grinned as he carried in the two cardboard boxes of pizza. "Umm," he said, "smells good."

Cara felt happier just being with him. And the smells of cheese, pepperoni, and tomato sauce wafting through the pizza boxes helped even more.

They headed for the arched front door of their Spanish house. "Why don't you girls eat outside on the patio?" Mom suggested.

"Okay," Cara agreed. "Why not?"

Dad handed her a Flicks plastic bag. "I brought three new videos, in case you and Jess want to watch. They're supposed to be good."

"Thanks," Cara said. "Thanks a lot." Knowing him, they wouldn't be anything like what Paige had left for her. The main reason he'd started Flicks was to provide decent family videos, which meant not dirty or violent.

After a while, Cara and Jess settled outside at the glass-topped patio table with their Cokes and a Morelli's Deluxe Pizza—pepperoni, mushrooms, onions, sausage, green peppers, and thick, thick cheese. "Ummmmm," Cara said.

"Ummmmm is right," Jess answered.

The pizza was already cut, and they helped themselves to slices, stringing out the cheese.

"Tricia and Becky don't know what they're missing," Jess said, taking a big bite.

"I guess not," Cara answered. She bit into a slice, but it didn't taste as good as usual.

"Look, Angora is watching us through the sliding glass door," Jess remarked.

"Yeah. She's nosey, but she stays her distance." It occurred to Cara that sometimes she was as much of a fraidycat herself as Angora.

They didn't talk much, so while she munched on her pizza she put her mind to what she'd write in her journal. Maybe something like, *It was a lovely night with birds twittering in the trees and the sun disappearing in an orangey-purple sunset behind the back wall*. To be truthful, she'd have to add, *But it hurt a lot to have Tricia and Becky leave*.

Well, she and Jess would get even with them later. Acting so high and mighty, they really deserved it.

At ten o'clock, they headed out through the darkness, each

carrying a flashlight and a plastic grocery bag with three rolls of white toilet paper.

"Yipes!" Jess yelped when she tripped over a stepping-stone in the darkness and barely caught her balance.

"Shhhhh!" Cara warned. Mom probably wouldn't care if they went out TP-ing Becky's and Tricia's yards; she'd think it was a good joke. But Dad was old-fashioned about lots of things—and one of them was respecting other people's property. Luckily they were watching TV in their bedroom so Jess and Cara could have the living room TV.

Stars and a half-moon lit the night, and outdoor lights glowed here and there in front of houses, so it was easy to see their way down the street. After a while, Cara quietly suggested, "Let's start at Becky's house since her house is farthest, then hit Tricia's to make a faster getaway."

"Good idea," Jess said. "Becky's dog is so old she won't hear us, but Tricia's might."

The front light was on at Becky's, but the rest of her house was dark, which could mean she'd gone to stay with Tricia, who was her best friend anyway. Becky's mother, a widow, might be out on a date with Mr. Bradshaw again. If so, Becky's grandmother, who had a condo near the beach, was there baby-sitting Becky's little sister, Amanda.

Next door, Tricia's house was dark, too. "Looks like nobody's home," Cara whispered to Jess.

"Come on!" Jess whispered back with a giggle. "It's the perfect time to strike!"

Cara put her flashlight down on the sidewalk, then ran across the grass toward the two pepper trees in Becky's front yard.

Jess called back softly, "Watch me!"

In the moonlight, Cara saw her unroll a long length of toilet paper, then toss the roll toward the top of the tree. It caught on the higher branches, then unrolled in the moonlight like a ghostly ribbon, tumbling down toward Cara's head. "Whoa!" she laughed, dodging away.

"Shhhh!" Jess warned. "Even if they're gone, the neighbors might hear."

Cara smothered a giggle as she unrolled the paper, then threw the roll up at the other tree. It caught halfway up, then unreeled so quickly that she had to run to catch it. "Fun!" she whispered, though she felt guilty. As she threw the roll up again, she stepped into a rut in the lawn and almost fell backwards. "Yii!" she yelled.

From behind the house, Lass, the Hamilton's old collie, gave a loud "Woof!"

"Run for it!" Cara whispered. She could imagine the scene already: a Santa Rosita police car after them, siren wailing. Sometimes kids got into real trouble—

"We're not leaving yet," Jess hissed and froze into position, listening. A full minute passed. "I think she's more grouched at being disturbed than anything. If we're quiet, she'll settle back to sleep."

"You sure?" Cara asked under her breath. Lass's doghouse was out back and, like most backyards in the neighborhood, it was fenced in. Lass couldn't bite them or anything, but she sure could wake up everyone.

"Cool it," Jess said.

Cara drew a nervous breath. "All right."

Standing in the shadows, they waited.

Lass was quiet, and after another minute passed, Jess, and then Cara began to giggle nervously.

"Shhhhh!" Jess hissed.

Holding back their giggles, they finished TP-ing Becky's front yard, then headed next door for Tricia's.

It was a two-story house, and Cara had a strange feeling— as if someone were watching them. She glanced up, but the half-open windows were dark. "Let's do it!" she whispered.

After looping the white streamers of paper out front, they edged nearer to the house to decorate the bushes.

PLOP! PLOP! PLOP!

Water balloons fell from a second-story window, bursting all around them—and one landed on Cara's head. It hurt as it smacked against her scalp. "Ow!" she yelped.

"We knew you two would be after revenge!" Tricia called down from her bedroom window. She and Becky threw another barrage of water balloons. "Now we'll let Chessie out after you!" she yelled. "Get 'em, Chessie!"

As if on cue, their big golden retriever began to bark loudly from behind the front door.

"Run!" Jess yelled as a balloon burst on her back. "Run like anything!"

Drenched, they ran to the street and grabbed their flash-lights. As if things weren't bad enough, a car's headlights filled the street. They ducked behind the nearest bushes, and Cara watched the car approach. It looked more and more familiar as it neared them . . . *Paige! It was Paige in her Thunderbird! If she saw them and what they'd done, it'd really make a mess of everything!*

CHAPTER

3

When Cara awakened the next morning, Jess was already dressed in her damp white shorts and T-shirt. She sat on the floor, tying the laces on her running shoes.

"Go back to sleep," Jess said. "It's only six. I'm going jogging."

"Uffff," Cara answered, rolling over in bed. She'd been so upset that she had hardly slept, and she didn't even want to remember what the trouble had been. The only good thing about it was that Paige hadn't seen them.

When Cara awakened again, Jess was gone—and so were her friend's sleeping bag and other things. Probably she was mad at her now, too.

Dejected, Cara climbed out of bed. Her room didn't look nearly as cheerful this morning. She drew a deep breath and reached under her mattress, where she kept her journal hidden. She panicked for an instant when she didn't feel it, then her fingers touched its hard cover.

Thank goodness for that! she thought as she tugged out the brown journal. She took a pen from the pencil mug on her desk and sat down on her bed and wrote,

June 28

Last night was one of the worst times of my life. This morning I still hurt too much inside to even cry. The trouble started with playing Paige's stupido video—which I didn't know was R-rated until later. Now I've probably lost my best friends and ruined the Twelve Candles Club. Why didn't I tell them I was sorry? Why did I have to be so stubborn?

I don't even know how to explain myself. Fine writer I am. The kids' writing magazine I read at the library says we should be able to explain our every feeling, so I'll try. I guess it happened because I didn't know what to do. Then I got surprised . . . and mad . . . and . . . I don't know what all else. Sometimes I think it's my shyness that causes lots of trouble. Shyness is supposed to be a fear of other people, but my problem seems more that when things go wrong, I don't know what to do, and then I get mad, too.

Now I don't know if I should show up this morning for washing cars or for the Tucker party this afternoon. I don't feel like facing Becky or Tricia, but I promised. If only I hadn't. I guess the worst that can happen is that they won't speak to me ever again.

At eight-thirty, she decided to ride her bike down the street to the Hutchinsons', who lived halfway between her house and Tricia's and Becky's. The Hutchinsons' dusty cars—a tan Mercury and a white Honda—were already parked in the driveway by their pale yellow two-story house. And there were Becky and Tricia, uncoiling a garden hose, their bikes parked near the garage.

The moment Cara rode into the driveway, she knew they saw her. Her eyes slid by them. "Hi," she mumbled.

Tricia and Becky stopped working and answered with a stiff "Hi."

Cara jumped down from her bike, then busied herself with its kickstand as she parked it near their bikes. If they weren't friendly, she'd ride right back home.

When she turned, she was startled to see them trying hard to smile at her.

Tricia stepped forward. "Despite everything last night, we hope you're still our friend. That's even more important than our old club."

Tears flooded Cara's eyes and she nodded. "I'm sorry. I'm really sorry."

"We are, too," Becky answered in a tone that showed she meant it. "We figured Paige talked you into playing that movie, and once you had it going, you didn't want to . . . you know, back down."

Cara nodded again, blinking hard to keep from crying. "You can be sure I'll never play any video Paige suggests again. We're supposed to send R-rated stuff right back, but I guess Paige must have been helping out and saw it . . . and wanted to make trouble."

"You think she did it on purpose?!" Becky asked.

"I think so," Cara decided. "Anyhow, I wouldn't be surprised. She's changed lately somehow."

Tricia hooked her long reddish-blond hair behind her ears thoughtfully. "It can't be easy sometimes, having Paige Larson for a sister."

"It isn't lately," Cara admitted.

Tricia gave her a little smile. "Well, God wants us to forgive others—and I sure forgive you."

Cara swallowed hard and looked down through a blur of tears at the concrete driveway. "Thanks."

"I forgive you, too," Becky added softly. "I thought you didn't really care about us or the club until I saw you ride up this morning. Then I knew it was just angry words, like when I get mad at Amanda for doing some dumb five-year-old thing, and after a while, I realize I love her after all."

"It was like that, all right," Cara agreed.

"Please forgive us for our part in wrecking your party," Tricia added. "Everything just turned into a mess."

Cara nodded. Probably she should tell them she forgave them, but it seemed too late now. Besides, maybe things would go back to how they were without getting into forgiveness, since she didn't know much about it.

Suddenly a new thought hit. "What about . . . what about our TP-ing your yards?"

Tricia grinned. "It's all cleaned up already. That part of last night and the water balloons were fun. In case you're wondering, we heard Lass bark and, knowing Jess, we guessed what was up."

Cara had to smile herself. "You know what made her bark? I stepped backwards into a rut and yelled."

Tricia gave a laugh. "Anyhow, the water balloons were fun. You must have been drenched."

"We were, thanks to you! Drenched to the skin."

Just then Mrs. Hutchinson stepped out the front door to put a letter into her mailbox.

"Guess we'd better get busy," Becky whispered. She'd already filled a plastic bucket with warm sudsy water. "Let's wash these cars and try to forget the bad stuff."

Cara hoped they really could forget the bad stuff on the video. "Thanks. Thanks a whole lot."

She began to fill a bucket with water from the hose, too. As the water swirled up in the bucket, she asked, "What do you mean, you're supposed to forgive?"

Tricia and Becky glanced at each other. After a moment, Tricia said, "God tells Christians that we have to forgive others, no matter what they do to us."

"No matter what they do? No matter how bad it is?"

Becky nodded. "No matter what, because God forgives us. Hey, why don't you go to Sunday school with us tomorrow morning? I think it'd help you a lot in your troubles with Paige. It sure helps me with Amanda."

"Maybe," Cara answered, squeezing out her soapy sponge. She'd be glad for *anything* that might help her with Paige. "I'll have to ask my parents. They might not like . . . I mean, they might have other plans."

Moments later, when Jess rode up on her bike, they were already hard at work. "Whoa! Fifteen cars to wash, the Tuckers' party this afternoon—and I'm late!" she exclaimed. "Don't worry, I'll make up for it."

Glancing at her, Cara wondered if she'd mention last night, but Jess set to work as if nothing had gone wrong.

Cara ran the soapy sponge over the white Honda. Maybe things hadn't been so bad after all. Maybe she was just like her mother said—overly sensitive.

At one-thirty, Cara rushed home and slapped together a peanut butter and tomato sandwich, then sat down on a stool at the white-tiled kitchen counter. Sometimes she wished that her mother would be home at lunch or when she came home from school, maybe baking an apple pie. Sometimes imagining what it would be like helped to make her feel better.

She was finishing her glass of milk when Paige stepped into the kitchen archway and struck a sleek modeling pose. "Well, what did your little friends think of *Moonstreams*?"

"Not much. We only saw the beginning and that was bad enough."

Paige smiled like an old Cheshire cat and headed for the refrigerator.

"You lied, Paige! You said it was PG–13, and you knew it was R! Why did you do it?"

Paige studied the contents of the refrigerator. "A mere test of you and your little friends."

"Stop calling us little!" Cara snapped. "We're old enough to work at the Tuckers' pool party this afternoon, helping to serve over one hundred people!"

Paige poured herself a glass of lemonade, then closed the refrigerator door. "Guess I'll get to see the famous Twelve Candles Club in action. I'll be at the party with Brad Tucker."

"You're invited?! They said it'd be all grown-ups."

"I *am* almost seventeen, and Brad is in college," Paige said. "Besides, we won't stay long, and it'll probably be boring-boring-boring."

Cara felt sick. Paige would watch her every move. She had a feeling that with her half sister there, the party would be a disaster for sure.

The wall phone rang, and since Paige had her own phone, Cara reached over to pick it up. "Hernandez residence," she answered. If it were Dad or Mom calling from Flicks, she'd better ask about going to Sunday school with Tricia and Becky.

No! Bad idea. With Paige around, she'd better wait or she'd never hear the end of it.

"Cara, it's me, Jess. The Tuckers decided they want us earlier. Can you be ready at four?"

"Sure," Cara answered. "I just have to wash my hair."

"Meet at my house," Jess said. "Mom will drive us."

"Okay, I'll be there."

Without them, she knew she'd never work at a job like this. Crowds of people—and sometimes only one or two—made her feel shyer than ever, almost shaky.

At four-thirty, Cara climbed out of Mrs. McColl's Mercedes with the others. Jess's mother warned, "I told Mr. Tucker that the Twelve Candles Club girls are experienced. Keep in mind that he's my boss. Don't let me down."

"We won't," Cara promised with Becky and Tricia.

"We can't!" Jess said. "If we're not good, everyone in Santa Rosita will hear about it. Maybe even everyone in California! It'd ruin our party-helper work for sure."

"Well, you all look wonderful," Mrs. McColl told them as she got ready to drive off. "Those gold candle medallions around your necks make you look like real winners, like Olympic stars."

Cara glanced at the others. They wore matching white skirts and blouses, and the club candle medallions hung around their necks, too. They did look special, just right for a working club. And they were all going to Sunday school tomorrow at Santa Rosita Community Church—even Jess! When Cara had asked her mom, she'd only said, "That's up to you," and Cara had answered, "Guess I'll try it once."

"Here we are," Jess announced.

Cara snapped back to attention and took a good look at the Tucker house. It was all glass and dark wood, and it sprawled over a huge lot covered with green grass, clusters of colorful flowers, and perfectly trimmed bushes and trees. The horse stables Mrs. McColl had told them about were probably out behind the house.

"Expensive," Jess remarked. "They act sort of snobby." She led them along a pebbly sidewalk toward the distant front door. "There, over by the garage . . . that's Mr. Tucker. Looks like he's telling the valet service where to park the cars." She gave a laugh. "Maybe even how to drive them!"

Mr. Tucker was short and potbellied all right, just as Jess had said. Cara's eyes went to his hair. "He doesn't look like he wears a toupee."

Jess grimaced fiercely, her hazel eyes bugging out. "Whoa! Nobody's supposed to know about it! Don't even say *the T-word*. Don't even think it!"

"Sorry," Cara apologized.

"It's okay," Jess said. "It's just that he thinks he's handsome. What he needs is a good mirror."

Tricia let go with a crazy giggle, and Cara gave a little laugh herself.

"Oh, no!" Becky groaned, then pointed toward the delivery driveway. "It's Wurtzel's catering van! Mrs. Wurtzel will be furious to see us working at another one of her jobs. Remember when she accused us of stealing the purses at Mrs. Llewellyn's dinner party?"

"Do I!" Jess answered. "I think she gets mad because she doesn't make as much money when she can't bring her own workers."

Just then Mr. Tucker saw them heading for the front door.

"Around back, girls," he barked. "Walk through the house . . . from the entry to the family room's doors. Mrs. Tucker is out back giving instructions to the caterer."

"Thanks," Jess answered. "We're on our way." She added under her breath, "He has a bossy voice."

"That he does," Tricia agreed. "If he were an actor, he'd make a good army sergeant."

"He was a general!" Jess said, almost laughing. "I should have told you, he's really General Tucker."

"I thought he was your mom's boss," Cara said. "You know, a real estate broker."

"He is," Jess answered, "but he's a retired general. Mom says we should call him General Tucker."

"Well, he sounds like a sergeant," Tricia insisted. "You know, the guy who barks out, 'Left . . . right . . . about face!' and all of that."

They all covered their mouths to muffle their laughter.

They were nearing the house, and Cara whispered, "We'd better be quiet. You know, not let anyone overhear us."

"Shhhh," Tricia and Jess whispered, crossing their eyes and knock-kneeing their legs like perfect klutzes. They almost laughed out loud before they stepped into the house, which was an awesome sight.

Flowers filled the entry, and Cara caught a glimpse of huge white couches in the living room. She hurried along with the others through a wood-paneled family room filled with silver trophies. "Hey, look—they have merry-go-round horses up by the ceiling!"

"Mrs. Tucker is horsey," Jess explained. "You know, she rides at horse shows all over. That's how she got all those trophies. See that quilt hanging on the wall? It's ribbons for winning at horse shows, all sewn together."

"How do you know so much about it?" Tricia asked.

"Mom took me to a horse show where Mrs. Tucker was riding," Jess explained. "They rode around and jumped hurdles. It would have been less boring if they'd stood on their heads or done cartwheels."

"Only you'd think of that, you gymnastic wacko!" Tricia said, and they all laughed in agreement.

Outside, the spacious covered patio was lined with buffet tables. Farther out around the pool, there were round tables topped by blue umbrellas.

"Ah, there you are, girls!" a tall, thin woman called out. She stood with Mrs. Wurtzel by the buffet tables.

"That's Mrs. Tucker," Jess told them.

It occurred to Cara that Mrs. Tucker had a horsey sort of face and neck, too. It was especially noticeable with her pale blond hair swept up into a coiled bun. She looked nice, though, in her fluttery flowered dress.

She waved them over to the buffet tables. "Mrs. Wurtzel says she already knows you. She'll be giving you your instructions." Mrs. Tucker eyed them sternly. "It's against my better judgment to have such young girls working at a party, but my husband made the arrangements while I was out of town last month."

"We'll do our best," Jess promised.

"You'd better!" Mrs. Tucker said firmly. She turned to Mrs. Wurtzel. "They're in your charge now."

Cara did not have a good feeling about it.

As soon as Mrs. Tucker clicked away in her white high-heeled sandals, Mrs. Wurtzel glared at them like a dark thundercloud. She wore her usual black dress and a ruffled white apron, and her dyed hair was blacker than ever. "Looks like I'm stuck with you girls again," she grouched. "How you get some of these jobs, I don't know."

Cara shrank back. She almost expected Tricia or Becky to say, "We pray a lot," since you never knew when they'd say it, but they didn't.

"Well," Mrs. Wurtzel began again, "you know what you did at Llewellyns' outdoor party . . . hand around appetizers, keep everythin' neat 'n clean, serve water, clear tables . . . then after it's over, wash dishes 'n clean up the whole mess. They wanted Mexican food, so it's tostadas, enchiladas, beans, rice, 'n the rest of it." She shot a suspicious look at Cara. "Don't know what they see in Mexican food myself. As if that ain't enough, they're puttin' a Mexican *mariachi* band back there, behind the buffet, to blast my ears out."

Cara drew a quiet breath and held it while the woman glared down at her. She guessed Mrs. Wurtzel didn't like Hispanics much, and she was probably wondering right now if Cara was one of them. For an instant, she was tempted to say Mom was an Anglo, but that she wouldn't exchange her Mexican father for anything.

"Well," Mrs. Wurtzel said again, still huffed up. She glanced around, then began to give orders. "Put them yellow napkins in them Mexican baskets, then dump in tortilla chips from them bags. You'll be servin' hot salsa, so keep them water pitchers filled. You can finish settin' tables, too."

"I'll finish setting tables," Cara offered, eager to get as far away as possible.

Mrs. Wurtzel squinted at Cara for a moment, then said, "Silverware and napkins are in that big basket." She cocked her head and heard the mariachi band tuning up out front.

"Hurry up, before we have to put up with that racket back there."

Cara rushed off.

The mariachi band sounded wonderful, she decided, no matter what Mrs. Wurtzel said. As for her suspicious look, probably she thought she'd steal the silverware. Well, Mrs. Wurtzel didn't have to worry. Tricia and Becky had been so forgiving this morning that Cara Hernandez was not going to let Wurtzel Catering—or even Miss Paige Larson—ruin any chances for the Twelve Candles Club!

CHAPTER

4

*B*y five o'clock, Cara had finished setting the fourteen round tables that surrounded the huge swimming pool. The tables were a colorful sight: blue tablecloths matching the blue umbrellas overhead . . . yellow and orange napkins standing up like tents . . . bouquets of blue, orange, and yellow crepe paper flowers. Around the edge of the pebbly patio, bright piñatas hung from the trees.

Out by the front of the house, the mariachi band played lively music, and guests began to stream into the Tuckers' spacious backyard.

Fiesta! Cara thought, enjoying the moment. The colors and joyous mariachi music turned the scene into a real fiesta. As for the swimming pool, she wished she could take a long swim. Swimming was one thing she did well, thanks to lots of summers of neighborhood Red Cross swimming classes.

Suddenly Mrs. Wurtzel stood before her frowning. "What

you doin', girl, starin' at the tables? Start offerin' the salsa, guacamole, and chips. Get movin'! Mind yer manners and remember yer place! This ain't yer party and don't forget it!"

Guests turned to glance at them, and Cara felt a blush race up her neck and to her cheeks. She hurried to the buffet and picked up a wooden tray that held bowls of salsa, guacamole, and tortilla chips. Her "place," as Mrs. Wurtzel called it, was to be hired help.

Cara put on a smile, made her way to a group of guests, and offered, "Salsa, guacamole, tortilla chips?"

"Don't you girls look nice in your white outfits?" one of the ladies remarked as she helped herself to a chip with salsa. "So much nicer than most waiters who work parties. I'll have to get your phone number for my next party."

"Thank you," Cara answered, a real smile spreading across her face.

After a while, the mariachis strolled around to the backyard playing "Spanish Eyes," which Cara loved since people often said she had beautiful brown eyes. As she moved on, she saw Jess, Becky, and Tricia walking around with their trays among the guests. They really did look good in their outfits, she thought, proud of the Twelve Candles Club.

"Well, if it isn't *Caro-leen-a Hernandez!*" a voice said from behind her, and Cara knew that her sister had arrived.

She turned and shot Paige a look that said "Stop it!"

Paige only smiled. Her blond hair shimmered in the sunlight, and she wore a new black and white sundress. Guests turned to stare at how beautiful she was, as well as notice that she held on to Brad Tucker's arm.

It was the first time Cara had seen him, and she didn't know what Paige saw in him. He was tall with slightly long blond hair, and sort of horsey-looking like his mother. On second thought, Paige probably liked him because he was in college and had lots of money.

"So that's your little sister," he said to Paige.

"Don't let it get around," Paige muttered.

"She doesn't look anything like you—"

"I hope *not!*" she replied.

Cara tried to smile as she held the tray toward them. "Salsa, guacamole, tortilla chips?"

"You know I can't stand Mexican food," Paige snapped. "Besides, I see that two of the other girls are offering crab and shrimp. Come on, Brad."

As they turned and left, Cara tried not to mind, but it hurt. She told herself she should have expected Paige to be nasty, that by now she should be used to it. And it wasn't too surprising, either, that Mrs. Wurtzel had stuck her with serving salsa, guacamole, and tortilla chips! Unhappily, she moved on through the guests.

Later, she saw Paige and Brad at the punch bowl with some of his college friends. General Tucker was there, too, proudly introducing his son Brad, as well as Paige, to his friends. In the sunlight, Cara noticed that the general's toupee was blacker than the rest of his hair. What's more, he was always touching it as if to make sure it was still on his head.

By six o'clock, the backyard was crowded with chattering guests, including Jess's parents. "Salsa, guacamole, tortilla chips?" Cara offered for the umpteenth time as she edged along through the crowd.

"Yes, thank you," Mr. and Mrs. McColl answered, then scooped salsa and guacamole onto chips while she waited.

"You girls are doing wonderfully," Mrs. McColl said. "I'm really proud of you."

"Thanks," Cara answered. "We won't let you down."

Mr. McColl gave a nod. "I can see that."

Cara excused herself, deciding she'd better go to the guests seated at the tables. They weren't eating dinner yet, just sitting down to visit and drink punch. They sat back in comfort, their chairs pushed too close together between the tables, and she had to raise her tray high to squeeze through between a fat man seated at one table, and Mrs. Tucker behind him. *Why can't they pull their chairs in?! You'd think Mrs. Tucker, as hostess, would notice.*

Suddenly Paige stepped up from behind her and whispered, "Have a good trip, *Caro-leen-a!*" as she hooked a foot around Cara's and jerked it hard.

Cara let out a surprised "Ufffff!" and lurched forward, trying to steady the tray overhead. At the last instant, she caught her balance, but not before salsa slopped off the tray and onto Mrs. Tucker's upswept blond hair.

"I'm sorry!" Cara gasped, horrified. "I'm so sorry!"

Mrs. Tucker touched her hair and felt the glob of tomato and onions trapped in her coiled bun. "Ohhhhh!" she uttered in disgust. She turned a poisonous look on Cara.

"I really am sorry!" Cara apologized, her face hot with embarrassment. "I didn't do it on purpose. . . ."

Nearby, guests stopped talking and watched, and Mrs. McColl put a hand to her mouth in shock.

"Hmmmpphhh," Mrs. Tucker huffed. She rose to her feet, trying to pretend nothing was wrong. "If you'll excuse me. . . ." With that, she rushed into the house, her flowery dress fluttering behind her.

Jess passed by with her tray. "What happened?"

"Paige tripped me," Cara whispered. She used napkins to wipe up the salsa all over her tray. She felt like crying, but refused to let herself. She knew what would happen, though: Mrs. Tucker would tell all her friends, and they'd never want to hire the Twelve Candles Club again.

Cara and Jess glanced at Paige, who'd just returned to Brad Tucker and his friends on the other side of the pool. She smiled right at them, looking perfectly innocent.

"Isn't Miss Paige Larson something!" Jess remarked.

Cara nodded. "What if Mrs. Tucker tells me to leave?"

"She won't," Jess said. "It would make her look bad. Keep on smiling and doing your best. Better get a fresh bowl of salsa, too."

Cara gave another nod and moved on. She'd work on the other side of the patio so she wouldn't have to face Mrs. Tucker again. Maybe everyone else would forget.

When she arrived at the buffet, Mrs. Wurtzel glared at her. "What you tryin' to do, ruin the party?"

"I didn't do it on purpose. I was tripped," Cara said. "I need more salsa—"

Mrs. Wurtzel's face turned cloudier than ever, and just then, General Tucker stepped behind the long buffet table with them, pretending to be there for more punch. "Young lady, watch what you're doing!" he warned Cara.

"I will, General Tucker. It—it was an accident."

He eyed her suspiciously. "Don't let it happen again."

"It won't, I promise. I'm really sorry."

Frowning, he overfilled his cup from the huge glass punch bowl in front of them and slopped red punch onto the patio. "Now look what you've made me do!"

Cara was sure that the guests all around were watching, and General Tucker must have noticed too, for he said, "Very well! Dismissed!"

She looked up at him, unsure if that meant she was to go home or if it was military talk meaning he was done talking to her. She stared at him and waited. From the corner of her eye, she saw Mr. and Mrs. McColl watching, too.

He patted his black toupee again, and at that very moment, Mrs. Wurtzel turned, bumped into him, and slipped on the spilled punch. Her feet went out from under her, and she grabbed the general's neck just as he raised his hand for a final "pat." His neck jerked sideways, his hand reached for the table, and suddenly he let out a yelp as his toupee went sailing through the air like a great hairy bird. It flopped into the punch bowl with a splash.

Mrs. Wurtzel's eyes almost popped from her head. She steadied herself and stood up straight, then pointed a bony finger at Cara. "It's her fault. That girl made me bump you! I knew from the beginnin' she'd be trouble."

His face red, General Tucker glared at Mrs. Wurtzel and made a revolted grunt. Then he reached into the punch bowl, fished out his toupee, and slapped it, dripping wet, back onto his head. Red punch trickled down his face, turning it redder yet.

Around them, guests burst into laughter. Cara clapped a hand to her mouth, at first in alarm, but then to keep from laughing herself. Nearby, the McColls couldn't help laughing with everyone else.

General Tucker tried to be a good sport as he stood there, red punch dripping from his nose. He grabbed a handful of napkins and patted first his face, then his sideburns, then the top of his head. He managed somehow to push his toupee to one side, and a red-stained bald patch appeared over his left ear. "Well," he said, "this will make for a memorable party. First Mrs. Tucker's hair and now mine." He grinned a little. "I bought it, so I guess I can call it mine."

The guests laughed harder, especially Brad and his college friends. Even Paige finally realized that it must be funny and joined in.

Someone said, "I didn't realize you'd hired these girls as part of a comedy routine."

The general nodded, trying to look amused, and Cara grabbed a bowl of salsa and rushed off. *What next?* she wondered. *The party is turning into a disaster—and it's my fault.* Why did she think she could ever be a party helper when people made her so nervous?

As she hurried to the far end of the patio, Tricia whispered, "Smile like everything's fine. None of it's been your fault, so s-m-i-l-e! Becky and I are praying for you. God can fix things."

"Fix this? General and Mrs. Tucker are furious with me."

"God can fix it," Tricia insisted.

Cara pasted on a frozen smile, but she felt more like crying. Even God couldn't get her out of this!

After a while, though, Mrs. Tucker returned with her hair slightly damp but perfect, and General Tucker's toupee stopped dripping. The mariachi band played and the guests were so busy talking that everyone seemed to forget.

Cara's smile was just returning when Mrs. Wurtzel told her to fill the water glasses at the tables. "Let's hope that keeps you out of trouble!" she grouched. "The other girls can help me serve from the buffet. I sure ain't trustin' it to you. And don't spill the water all over the tables!"

Cara grabbed two water pitchers and fixed her mind on the mariachi music and filling the glasses with care. If only she were at home in bed!

Before long, the guests lined up at the long buffet tables to heap their plates with food. Now it was only a matter of cleaning up punch cups and little napkins, Cara told herself. Soon she could escape!

From the corner of her eye, she saw Brad Tucker being lectured by a plump elderly lady he called Aunt Hattie. They stood by the deep end of the pool, away from everyone else, and she shook her finger like she meant to talk some sense into him—for once and for all time to come. Cara heard parts of what she said . . . "girls of her sort" and "tripping that nice little waitress. . . ."

Aunt Hattie waved her arms as she spoke, and Brad backed away, moving closer to the pool with each step. "Don't be a fool, Brad!" she warned him.

He took one more backward step, panicked as he saw the water and tried to catch himself, then splashed straight into the pool, his head hitting the edge of the diving board with a clunk.

For an instant, Cara refused to believe it had happened, then she saw him going down in the water—and he wasn't swimming! Worse, everyone at the buffet was chattering loudly over the loud music. Only Aunt Hattie seemed to know what had happened, and she just stood there, horrified.

Not me! Cara thought. *I don't want to save him!*

In a flash, she saw there was no one else. She jerked off her sandals, dashed to the deep end, and dove in. When she came up through the water, it took only a moment to find him. She grabbed his hair and pulled with all of her might to get him to the surface.

"Help!" she yelled.

But the few who noticed seemed stunned, glued in place. At last someone yelled, "Call the paramedics!"

Cara swam along with her arm looped around Brad's head, just like she'd learned in the swimming class for lifesaving, pulling him toward the shallow end while the guests came running.

At the shallow end, he coughed up lots of water and slumped unsteadily on the pool steps. Finally he shook his wet blond head groggily, then touched the lump that rose on the back of his head. "How'd I get in the pool?" he mumbled.

"You backed in, trying to get away from me!" Aunt Hattie answered. "And that nice girl saved you! The very girl who's been quietly taking the blame for other people's actions!" She pointed at Cara. "That one."

Everyone turned to look at her, and Tricia started the applause, making Cara feel like hiding her head.

"We didn't even notice!" a guest exclaimed over the applause. "If it weren't for her, he might have drowned!"

Wacko as ever, Tricia yelled, "Encore! Encore!"

Cara tried not to smile, but after a day of disasters, applause sure was a nice change. She climbed out of the pool and felt a hot glow rush up to her cheeks. Her white blouse and skirt were dripping, and she pushed her hair away from her face. Suddenly it hit her. *Was this the answer to Tricia's and Becky's prayers to fix things? Had God given her a chance to do good?*

Paige stood by the pool steps, helping to hold Brad up. "Well," she huffed, "if it isn't the little heroine!"

"Not me," Cara answered, feeling shyer yet. She couldn't

believe all the wacko things that had happened: Paige making her spill salsa on Mrs. Tucker's hair, Mrs. Wurtzel blaming her for General Tucker's toupee falling into the punch bowl— and now, maybe even saving Brad Tucker's life!

Applause rang across the backyard now, and Jess yelled, "Yahoo!" Beside her, her parents clapped too.

Becky followed with, "Take a bow!"

Right in front of Cara, though, Paige looked furious. And instead of feeling proud, Cara felt more like jumping back into the pool.

CHAPTER

5

June 29

    Who'd ever believe what all happened to me yesterday? First of all, that Tricia and Becky would forgive me—and that even Jess would sort of forgive me too, in her own way? Anyhow, I ended up washing cars and working at the Tuckers' party with the Twelve Candles Club.

    And who'd believe what happened at the Tuckers' party?! First, I spilled salsa on Mrs. Tucker's hair, then Mrs. Wurtzel of dear old Wurtzel Catering blamed me for her bumping General Tucker and causing his toupee to fall into the punch bowl. Not only was I ready to die that very instant, but it looked like the Twelve Candles Club's party-helper reputation would be ruined forever and ever. For all eternity.

    Well, Tricia and Becky said they were praying for me, which isn't unusual. They're always praying anyhow. Then Brad Tucker—Paige's date—fell into the swimming pool and

I had to save him. And who should turn into the heroine of a hopeless mess, but me?

When the party ended, Mrs. Tucker gave us a bonus (!) and actually apologized for being so unpleasant when we first met her. And General Tucker took off his toupee and said, "No sense in wearing it now that everyone knows what I really look like." Even Brad thanked me for rescuing him. Only Paige and Mrs. Wurtzel looked like t-h-u-n-d-e-r-c-l-o-u-d-s. I'll bet Paige will be out for revenge.

Did God work out everything for me after it all looked so hopeless? Maybe. Anyhow, I might find out soon because in one hour I'm going to Sunday school. Would you believe it? My first time ever. Even if I don't like it, I figure a writer should learn about everything so she understands all kinds of people. That sounds very bold, when I'm actually feeling nervous about it. Anyhow, I guess it will be interesting. After rereading this, I think I should title this morning's writing, "Would You Believe?"

As far as that religion stuff goes, it's easy for me to believe in God when I look at Angora, who is sitting in the sunshine on my window seat. She is so beautiful, from her white fur right to her long whiskers. Besides her being a kind of miracle, I know when she sits in my lap and purrs that at least Angora Hernandez loves me.

And while I'm on that subject, I know that Dad really loves me. For one thing, he tells me so, but even without that, I'd know from the way he looks at me, and sometimes just from the way he calls me his "Amiga."

And I guess I know that, deep down inside, Mom really loves me, too.

It was a beautiful, sunny morning as they drove along in Mrs. Bennett's maroon minivan to the church, but Cara's hands felt as cold as the fear in her heart. Probably she shouldn't be going to Sunday school; probably she wouldn't even know most of the kids there.

She sat very still in the middle of the backseat since her pale yellow dress from last summer cut under her arms. For days, Mom had been promising to take her shopping, but she never had time. Cara was thankful she'd ridden her bike to the Shoe Stable to buy her white sandals with her own money. Her white purse from there was nice, too, she decided again, admiring its shell-like beads, some of which were sewn into four-petaled flowers.

Jess sat in the middle of the van's backseat, and Becky by the opposite window. Tricia occupied the middle seat with her seven-year-old sister, Suzanne. And Mrs. Bennett had made five-year-old Bryan sit up front with her to keep him under control.

Everybody was sleepy and quiet for a change, so Cara gazed out the window. Here along Ocean Avenue, palm trees swayed in the morning breeze and, compared to the usual traffic, there were only a few cars out and occasional joggers running on the sidewalks.

When they stopped for a red light, Mrs. Bennett glanced back at them with a smile. "You're all so quiet, I thought you must be asleep."

"I guess we're still tired from the Tuckers' party," Tricia answered. "It was hard work, especially the humongous cleanup."

"But a real sensation of a party," Becky added. "I'll never forget when General Tucker's toupee fell into the punch bowl and he slapped it right back on his head. And the red punch dribbling down his face!"

"It certainly sounds memorable," Mrs. Bennett laughed.

Everyone else laughed a little, and Tricia added, "The thing I'll never forget was Cara pulling Brad Tucker out of the pool. I wish we had a video of it. She did it just like they taught in Neighborhood Swim."

"I should think it'd be a sensation," Mrs. Bennett answered. "Cara, you're a real heroine."

"Not me," Cara protested, though she was half-pleased anyhow. Even now, it didn't seem possible that she'd actually done such a thing. Maybe Tricia or Jess would, or even Becky . . . but Cara Amelia Hernandez? It was unreal. No way. N-o w-a-y!

Mrs. Bennett sent her a fast smile in the rear-view mirror. "You never know when God wants to use us."

Cara's brain went on alert. There it was again about God using people! Had God gotten her to rescue Brad Tucker? If so, she hadn't even known it.

She felt Jess glance at her, too. Jess had gone to church with her father and brother, Jordan, once or twice, but she said it'd been too hard to understand some of it, so she was trying Sunday school this morning.

"Did God tell you to save Brad?" Jess asked.

Cara lifted her shoulders in a shrug. "I didn't hear a voice or anything like that."

Tricia's little sister, Suzanne, had been listening hard. Now she said, "God talks quietly, doesn't He, Mom? He talks in a still, small voice."

"Usually," Mrs. Bennett answered. "But He can speak to us any way He wants. After all, He's God . . . a God of wonders and miracles."

Cara guessed that Mrs. Bennett must know a lot about Him

since her father-in-law was a retired minister. It seemed strange, though, that she and her husband—a minister's son!—were separated. It was unusual for Tricia not to put in her opinion too, and Cara craned her neck around slightly for a better look at Tricia. Instead of being her usually dramatic self, she had her hands folded and her eyes closed. She was praying right here in the van in the middle of their conversation!

Jess's eyes met Cara's, and Jess gave a shrug, as if she didn't understand too much about it, either. Maybe they could find out things like that this morning.

The white stucco buildings of Santa Rosita Community Church were topped by red tile roofs and surrounded by lots of trees. Red geraniums bloomed around the bright green lawn. Already, cars jammed the parking lot, but a man waved them to what Mrs. Bennett called the "overflow lot," where there were still a few spaces.

"The Sunday school rooms are out back," Tricia told Cara and Jess as they climbed out of the van.

"Go on ahead," Mrs. Bennett told them. "I have to retie Bryan's shoelaces. I'll take him and Suzanne to their classes today. Have a good morning."

A good morning? Cara wondered, since she felt worried how it would turn out.

As they headed for the sidewalk, she and Jess hung back behind Tricia and Becky. "Don't worry," Jess said under her breath, "it was nice in the church last Sunday."

Cara let out a thankful breath. "Paige said she went to a church once, and it was boring-boring-boring."

"Sounds just like her," Jess said. "Seems to me Paige says boring-boring-boring about everything because she thinks it makes her look smart. But, is she an honor roll student like you? Has she ever gotten an A at school in her entire life?"

"No, I guess not," Cara answered. "I hadn't thought of that. She's not smart, but . . . you know what? . . . she's clever in sort of a devious way."

"You said it, not me!" Jess replied.

"Well, that's what Dad told Mom, so it's not my idea. Not that I haven't noticed it, though."

They'd walked past the big buildings and headed toward what looked like classrooms. "Here's where we start," Tricia said, leading the way into a big room. "It's everyone from seventh through ninth grade together at first. After a while, we go to our own rooms."

Stepping in, Cara looked around the large room. It was full of noisy kids, and she recognized some of them from school. They smiled as if they were really glad to see her and Jess. At least, that was okay.

"Let's sit in the middle," Becky suggested, heading for four empty chairs. "Here's song sheets for all of us. I remember the first time I came here two years ago and didn't know what to do, so I'll try to help you."

"Thanks," Cara told her, reassured.

"There's Bear," Tricia said, waving toward the front of the room. "He's our youth minister, and his real name is Ted. You know, Ted, as in Teddy Bear. Bear is so fun!"

He was short, broad-shouldered, and looked sort of like a cozy Teddy Bear all right, Cara decided. He wore baggy cotton pants and a flowered Hawaiian shirt. What's more, he'd brought along a guitar, which he now strapped around his neck. For some reason, she'd thought ministers would be formal and reserved—not be called Bear and smile from ear to ear. His blue eyes smiled, too.

"Good morning, gang," he said, strumming a chord on his guitar to quiet them down.

"Good morning, Bear!" they echoed cheerfully, as if they liked him.

He beamed at them. "Let's begin with a real uplifting song. The words are on your song sheets. 'Jacob's Ladder.' Get it? Ladder . . . uplifting?"

"Ohhhhh!" the older kids groaned laughingly.

Cara smiled herself as she found the words on the handout. Maybe this morning would be all right.

While he waited for them to find the song, he explained, "The phrase 'climbing Jacob's Ladder' has to do with our lives . . . climbing the rungs of life to heaven with Jesus as our helper."

He strummed a new chord, then sang with them,

We are climbing Jacob's ladder,
We are climbing Jacob's ladder,
We are climbing Jacob's ladder,
Soldiers of the cross.
Every rung goes higher, higher . . .

Cara tried to sing along with them, not knowing the tune or even who Jacob might be. She felt like a little kid, sitting with her mouth hanging open as she watched the other kids. Well, at least she could read the words.

When they finished all of the verses, Bear said, "If God seems far away to you, guess who moved?"

"We did!" the kids answered.

Does that mean God is closer than I thought? Cara wondered. *Not just faraway out in the universe? Maybe they'll explain it.*

"Right," Bear answered. "God's always ready to hear us

and to guide us. He wants to bless everyone. And, to do that, He wants you to be a blessing to others. But you can't be a blessing unless you're connected to God. The connection He sent us is Jesus."

Cara was beginning to understand more, but it was a lot to take in for her first time.

"God works through people," Bear added.

Mrs. Bennett had said something similar this morning, but what could that mean? Sometimes Tricia said she prayed to be used by Him. Becky too.

Bear strummed his guitar again. "Now how about singing one of my favorites, 'Bless the Lord.' "

Cara turned over the handout nervously and finally found the words. As they sang, she glanced at Tricia and Becky. They closed their eyes—and really meant it. She followed along on the song sheet, and it was almost as if the room changed, as though it had filled with a special sweetness.

"I see we have some newcomers here," Bear said after the song finished. "How about calling out your names so we can all get to know you?"

"Jess McColl," Jess announced, not a bit shy.

Jess turned to Cara, who said a quiet "Cara Hernandez."

From the back of the room, someone else called out a name.

"Welcome," Bear said. "We hope you'll have a fine time, maybe even learn a little, and come back again. Today, we're going to have a little skit. Jeff Palmer is going to go outside while I read you a scripture verse."

Jeff, a boy who had graduated with Cara's sixth-grade class from Santa Rosita Elementary, headed for the door and went out, closing it behind him with a grin.

Bear told them, "Jesus said this himself in Revelation 3:20.

I stand at the door and knock. If anyone hears my voice and opens the door, I will come in."

Bear turned to the door and waited, then someone—probably Jeff—knocked. "Let's not answer," Bear told them, and Jeff knocked on the door from outside again.

"Why doesn't Jesus just walk in after He knocks on the door of our hearts?" Bear asked.

"Because He doesn't force himself on anyone," Tricia answered. "You have to unlock the door of your heart to Him yourself."

"Exactly," Bear answered. "It's as if He doesn't want to use the knob on His side of the door, so we're the only ones who can open the door to let Him in." He walked over to the door and opened it wide. "I'll let you in, Jeff," Bear told him. "Just like every one of us has to let Jesus into his or her own heart. Any questions?"

Cara wasn't sure she understood, but she wasn't about to raise her hand. Maybe she'd ask Tricia later since she knew all about it.

"Now, how about a wet and wild, happy reminder to ourselves? Let's sing 'River of Life!' It's on the handout, if you don't know it."

He played his guitar and sang out with the kids,

I've got a river of life flowing out of me,
Makes the lame to walk, and the blind to see,
Opens prison doors, sets the captives free.
I've got a river of life flowing out of me.

Suddenly all the kids stood up and sang out, "Spring up, O well, SPLISH SPLASH!" and on the words "splish splash," flicked their fingers in the air, as if they were shaking water

63

everywhere. They did that three times in a row, sitting down after each "splish splash," until the whole group was laughing.

Cara was confused. She thought that church was supposed to be solemn and serious. Was it okay to have fun at church? And what did a river have to do with Jesus? She knew from singing Christmas carols that Jesus was God's Son, but it was hard to figure out what that had to do with kids her age having a "river of life" inside of them.

The second verse was about the well springing up in "my soul" and making "me whole" to give "that life abundantly." Cara tried to follow the words and the actions as if she knew them.

When they finished and all the kids settled into their seats again, Bear's face glowed with joy. "God loves it when we enjoy worshiping Him," he said. "He's not only our Savior, but also our Joy-giver, and when we know Him, we know His joy-smile."

It was hard to understand what joy had to do with her and God. Besides, how could anyone know His joy-smile, whatever that was. Or even know Him at all?

"You may all go to your classrooms," Bear told them, un-strapping his guitar. "All except seventh graders, who I'll be talking to today. Got that? Seventh graders stay. How about moving in closer to the front so I don't have to shout at you and wear out my poor old voice?"

Cara got up with her friends, and they moved to seats in the third row.

Bear sat backwards on a chair and smiled at them as they settled down again. "Well," he began, "you're now in junior high, which reminds me. Don't forget about the beach party for junior high kids. It's Tuesday, four o'clock until seven, at

Connor's Cove. You're all invited. See the details in the hand-out."

He drew a deep breath. "So then, this last year in Sunday school, you've been the oldest kids. Now, though, you're at the bottom of the heap here and at Santa Rosita Junior High or Santa Rosita Christian, or wherever else you might go.

"At school, you have peer pressure, and if you haven't heard about that, it means being pushed to be like others, even though God made you to be a s-p-e-c-i-a-l individual, not like any other person who's ever lived—that special! About this time every summer, I hear more complaints about a different kind of pressure, though. These come from home, not school. It's big sister, big brother, or even little sister, little brother pressures."

Cara swallowed. He wasn't looking at her, but it seemed as if he knew about her troubles with Paige. Did all of these other kids have problems like that, too?

Bear continued, "That's why it's important to know what God wants us to do instead of what others want us to do. What God wants us to do is what's good for us. What others want us to do is sometimes evil and will do us harm."

Like Paige talking me into showing that R-rated video, Cara thought.

"God gave us things like the Ten Commandments to help us," Bear said. "Now, most of us don't like rules, but I promise these will make a difference for good in your life."

Bear asked some kids to pass around a handout, and Cara took hers.

"Here they are," he said, then read from the handout. "First commandment: God says, 'I am the Lord your God, who brought you out of Egypt, out of the land of slavery. You shall have no other gods before me.' That means you don't make a god of your girlfriend or boyfriend or anyone else. What other things do people worship or make gods of?"

Kids raised their hands.

"Their talent, like art," Becky answered.

"Their work," someone else said. "Or football . . . or a hobby like some grown-ups do about travel. Or even money."

"Good," Bear said, then read again.

"Second commandment: 'You shall not make for yourself an idol in the form of anything in heaven above or on the earth beneath or in the waters below.' " Bear looked up at them. "Who can mention some of today's idols?"

Tricia raised a hand. "Rock stars, sports stars, movie stars, TV stars. . . ."

"Right," Bear answered.

He read again. "Third commandment: 'You shall not misuse the name of the Lord your God, for the Lord will not hold anyone guiltless who misuses his name.' Now what does that mean?"

Kids raised their hands, and one said, "Using His name in vain, like saying 'Oh, God!' or swearing."

"Or even using His name lightly," someone added.

Cara winced. No one had told her it was against God's rules, but she'd have to quit saying "Oh, God!" now. Not that she'd said it often like Paige.

"Number four: 'Observe the Sabbath day by keeping it holy, as the Lord your God has commanded you. Six days you shall labor and do all your work, but the seventh day is a Sabbath to the Lord your God.' " He looked at them. "How many of us go to church on Sunday then forget to honor God later in the day?"

A few hands went up, and Cara glanced at Tricia and Becky. So that was why they wouldn't take jobs on Sunday for the Twelve Candles Club.

"Number five," Bear continued. " 'Honor your father and your mother, as the Lord your God has commanded you, so that you may live long and that it may go well with you in the land the Lord your God is giving you.'

"We'll read the last five next week." He put down the hand-out. "Why are we to follow these commandments?"

"Because God told us to," a boy answered.

"And because they're for our own good," Tricia added.

"Right," Bear answered. "And to keep us from listening to peer pressure and paying attention to bad stuff from others?"

"Right!" everyone chorused.

Cara squirmed in her chair. No one had ever told her any of this. Sure, she knew it was bad to worship money and to be disobedient to your parents, but not that it was because God said so.

"There's another reason we should keep God's commandments in mind," Bear told them. "They keep us from getting involved with evil. You've probably all heard about the kidnapper who's been around our area. Now there's a sad example of a man with evil on his mind."

Did Bear really believe in evil?! Cara wondered. Well, she wasn't going to ask, but one thing she knew, she didn't want anything to do with it.

"Pleasing God is important because He cares about us," Bear said. "He loves us more than anyone else, and that's why

He's given us these commandments. To keep us from getting hurt."

It sounded as if God loved her even more than Angora did, Cara decided. So that's what she'd try to do—please God.

CHAPTER

6

When Cara returned home from Youth Group, the Flicks van was missing from the driveway. Mom and Dad were already at Flicks since Sunday was a busy day for video returns.

Sunday . . . the Sabbath! Should she tell them what the Bible said about it? You'd think they would know since Mom had attended Sunday school as a girl, and Dad had even been an altar boy in a church in Mexico. Hadn't they learned the Ten Commandments when they went?

As Cara unlocked the front door and headed down the hallway to her room, she noticed that Paige's door was open for a change. Her sister sat on her unmade bed, spreading lotion on her perfectly tanned legs. She wore a black sundress to match her red and black room. "Well, if it isn't the little Sunday school girl," Paige declared. "I suppose you'll be goody-good and sweety-sweet now, not to mention boring-boring-boring."

Cara stopped, then decided not to answer. After all, her parents hated their fighting, and she guessed it would please God if she pleased her parents.

Paige smirked. "What's the matter? Did God get your tongue?"

Cara let out an "Uffff!" and started for her room.

"You look absolutely stupid in that old yellow dress," Paige called out behind her. "Everyone there must have noticed it's too small for you."

"Shut up!" Cara shouted back, and immediately hated herself for fighting. But sometimes Paige made her so angry! "No one noticed my stupid dress," she seethed. "And you're not supposed to use God's name in vain!"

Paige capped the lotion and rose to her bare feet. "What *are* you jabbering about?"

"About your asking if God got my tongue," Cara retorted and stomped down the hallway.

Paige gave a laugh and followed her into the hallway. "That's using God's name in vain? My, my, how holy you are!"

Cara felt about as holy as a bum and was ready to back down as usual, until she remembered what Bear had said. She let out the words like a collapsing balloon. "It's using His name lightly."

"Who says we're not supposed to?"

"The Bible," Cara mumbled. She couldn't help adding, "And you're not supposed to lie, either." She hurried into her room and closed the door.

She'd no more than put the Sunday school handout on her chest of drawers, than Paige flung the door open.

"Listen, *Caro-leen-a Hernandez*, don't you ever-ever-ever tell me what I should or shouldn't do!"

70

Cara's heart began to pound. "Huh! You don't even know what I'm talking about, do you?" she sneered. "I didn't make it up—that's what it says in the Bible!"

A worried look flashed across Paige's face, but only for an instant. Then she raised her chin as usual when she didn't like something. "Is that so?"

"That's so," Cara answered.

"Why?"

"Tricia says it will open you up to evil."

"Evil-shmevil!" Paige retorted. "If that's what you learned in Sunday school, I'm glad I never went again!"

Cara shrugged. "You just don't want to hear about lying and other bad stuff."

Paige crossed her arms. "Just shut up."

"See, didn't I tell you?"

"Ohhh!" Paige shot back and flounced away.

It seemed that Paige had gone from bad to worse since she'd inherited the money and started hanging around with her snooty friends, Cara thought as she closed her bedroom door again.

She took a deep breath to calm down. When she turned, she saw Angora hunched against the shutters over the window seat. "Poor kitty." Angora had been kicked a time or two by Paige, who didn't like white fur on her clothes or her furniture, and it looked as if Paige had been after her again.

Knowing just how Angora felt, Cara went over to her and petted her until she purred and lay content in the sunshine.

Once Angora drifted off to sleep, and Cara had calmed down, she changed into her white shorts and a yellow T-shirt. More yellow to prove to Paige that she didn't always wear white. Besides, yellow was one of her favorite colors.

She dug her journal out from between the mattresses and got her pen from the pencil mug. Finding the last entry, June 29, she added,

Sunday noon

This morning at Sunday school was the first time I've learned anything much about God. Probably I'll go again if Tricia or Becky asks me. So far, though, I don't see how it's going to help me get along with Paige. Nobody could get along with her!

What I liked best about it was being with my friends and learning that maybe it was God who got me to jump into the pool to save Brad. The singing was all right, too, even though I didn't know any of it. And I guess learning the Ten Commandments is for people's own good. I liked Bear, too. He was all right for a grown-up.

If I go to the Sunday school beach party, I'll have to get a new bathing suit because my old one is faded, stretched out, and too small. The handout about the party says "modest swimsuits."

On the way home in the Bennetts' van, Tricia explained why Bear insisted on modest swimsuits. He says girls might wear skimpy bikinis because of peer pressure, meaning everyone else does it. Or because they think they look good in one. But boys don't see it that way. Boys see a girl in a skimpy bikini and think she's wild and will do a-n-y-t-h-i-n-g. I wonder if Paige knows that's what they think. She wears tiny bikinis.

Anyhow, I'm not sure yet if I'll go. I guess if I'm going to honor the Sabbath, I'll sit out in the yard and read in my poetry book that I bought at a used bookstore last month. Maybe I'll write some poetry, too.

Let's face it, I need a rest before tomorrow's Morning Fun

*for Kids! I'd never tell the others, but it's the one TCC job I
dread. I just don't know how to control so many little kids,
maybe because I don't have younger sisters or brothers myself.*

At four o'clock Mom phoned and asked Cara to start dinner. "Just make a salad and set the table," she said. "I'll bring
home frozen lasagna."

"Sure," Cara answered. She'd no more than hung up the
phone, though, than she remembered what Bear had read from
the Bible about honoring the Sabbath. One thing for sure, if
she said she couldn't set the table or make a salad on Sundays,
Mom wouldn't like it one bit.

What should I do, God? she asked.

She waited a long time, but there was no answer. She had
a feeling, though, that she'd better do what Mom said. That
was honoring her mother.

Later, at dinner, Cara said, "It was interesting to go to
Sunday school."

Mom's eyes narrowed. "Paige says you were preaching at
her. We don't mind your going to Sunday school, Cara, but
please keep it to yourself!"

Cara glanced at her father, but he kept his eyes down, eating
his salad. She couldn't believe it. What was the matter with
him? "I thought you were an altar boy at church—"

"Listen to your mother," he said, still not looking up.

She'd only heard five of the Ten Commandments and
couldn't even obey those. Ten commandments would be im-
possible. It seemed that she would never ever make a good
Christian.

At eight-thirty the next morning, she and Jess rode their

73

bikes to Tricia's house for Morning Fun for Kids. Probably it'd be best not to tell Jess what Mom and Dad had said about Sunday school and keeping her mouth shut, Cara decided. On the other hand, Jess's mother didn't go to church, either.

After a long time, Jess said, "You're quiet."

Cara shrugged as they pedaled along. "Let's hope the kids aren't as wild as usual this morning."

"You know it," Jess agreed. "There are twenty coming."

"Twenty!" Cara echoed. "The most we've ever had to handle was fourteen, and that was awful. How can we take care of twenty of them?"

"Who knows?" Jess sounded worried herself, and if *she* was concerned, there was definitely something to worry about.

Sometimes just thinking about those wild kids made Cara's heart pump like crazy. Probably it was hard for her to control little kids because she was too timid.

At least Tricia's peach-colored two-story house looked friendly and welcoming. As usual, Becky's sign hung on the Bennetts' breezeway gate. MORNING FUN FOR KIDS, PLEASE KNOCK ON GATE was lettered across the poster.

Cara jumped off her bike and, being taller than Jess, reached over on tiptoe to unlatch the gate. The latch was plenty high so little kids couldn't get to it.

She walked her bike in, Jess right behind her.

"We're here!" Jess announced.

"Thank goodness you're not late," Becky called back. She was setting out a craft project on the redwood table. "Tricia's getting into a pirate costume for the Magic Carpet."

Jess and Cara parked their bikes in the garage, then grabbed the big cardboard boxes the kids liked to use for cars, boats, trucks, airplanes, and spacecraft. They dragged them out, bumping them over the lawn.

Tricia's backyard was perfect for Morning Fun for Kids, Cara thought again as she dragged the two biggest cardboard boxes onto the lawn. There was a wooden play gym and sand-box, a tree house in the California pepper tree, and a solid wooden fence around the whole yard. Besides the redwood picnic table and benches for crafts, a clay tile water fountain stood in the breezeway for thirsty kids, and the pass-through shelf from the kitchen window was great for serving snacks. As usual, Butterscotch, the Bennetts' old cat, sat on the pass-through shelf watching them.

"How come twenty kids are coming?" Cara asked Becky.

"Some of the regulars are bringing neighbors and friends," Becky answered. She'd bought lots of brown fuzzy material on sale to use for making monkey puppets. "Let's hope I have enough material for the ones who want to do crafts."

Tricia jumped out the back door wearing a pirate costume. "Hey, mateys!" she called out, hoisting a long plastic sword that belonged to her brother, Bryan.

"You look fierce," Jess told her.

"Good!" Tricia laughed. "Maybe that'll help keep the kids under control." She turned to Cara. "There's another pirate outfit on the family room couch for you—"

"For me?" Cara repeated. Usually she just helped. She wasn't like Tricia, who did dramatic carpet rides, or Jess, who taught the kids gymnastics, or Becky with her arts and crafts talent. Mostly she was a go-fer, meaning, "go fer this" and "go fer that."

"Yep, a pirate outfit for you," Tricia answered. "With so many kids, I'll need another pirate on the back of the magic carpet to keep them in line. Everyone else's time is filled to the brim."

Cara had a feeling there wasn't much choice. "Just so I'm not the *chief* pirate."

One of Tricia's eyes was covered with a black pirate patch, but the other green eye sparkled. "I'm the *chief* pirate," she declared, then grinned. "Don't worry. It'll be fine. In fact, it might even be wonderful."

"All right." Cara swallowed hard and hurried for the family room's sliding door.

Inside, Suzanne and Bryan Bennett were watching *Old Yeller* on video with Becky's five-year-old sister, Amanda. Mrs. Bennett was probably getting dressed.

Cara saw the pirate outfit on the couch: baggy black pants, a tattered purple jacket, a black felt pirate's hat, and a black eye patch. She pulled the pants and jacket on over her shorts and T-shirt, then added the black eye patch like Tricia's and the black hat.

As she headed for the door, Bryan yelled, "Hey, another pirate! Ho, ho, ha, ha!"

"Ho, ho, ha, ha, yourself," Cara answered, trying hard to sound jolly, but sounding weird instead. "Aren't you kids coming outside?"

"As soon as everything's started," Suzanne Bennett answered. "We wanna finish watching *Old Yeller*. It's almost to the end."

"Oh," Cara said, uneasy as ever. She pulled her pirate hat down lower on her forehead, then went outside.

"Whoa, you look super!" Tricia exclaimed. "Now let's hear a hearty 'Ho, ho, ho, me mateys!' "

Cara drew a deep breath, then managed a weak, "Ho, ho, ho, me mateys!"

"Come on, you've got to do better than that!" Tricia said. "Just pretend you're a pirate and forget about quiet Cara Amelia Hernandez. Do you know any pirate tales?"

"Ummm . . . only 'The Pirate Story.' It's a poem. But I don't think I remember all of it."

"Just fill in where you forget."

"I can't recite to the kids like you do—"

"Cara Hernandez, you *can* if you'll try," Tricia argued. "Besides that, if God's given you the talent for communicating with words, He won't let you down if you trust Him and try!"

"You wouldn't make me, not today!" Cara said.

Tricia just grinned. "Ho, ha, ho!"

"You wouldn't—" But Cara had a feeling she would.

Out by the street, car doors began to bang, which made Cara swallow harder yet.

"Yipes, early Funners!" Jess exclaimed. "Quick, let's run through today's plan just one time."

Becky handed out the list, which wasn't too different than usual.

1. Magic Carpet game (Tricia & Cara). Becky and Jess blow up balloons for Balloon Fun.
2. Bean Bag Fun (Jess & Cara).
3. Gymnastics (Jess). Or crafts (Becky). (Tricia & Cara get out midmorning snacks.)
4. Midmorning Snacks (Tricia & Cara).
5. Free time for swings, playing with boxes, etc. (All except Becky who stays with crafts).
6. Sand castle contest. (All except Becky who stays with crafts.)

"It looks like plenty to do for three hours," Jess said.

Becky shrugged. "Except with lots of different Funners coming every time, you never know what might happen."

"You said it!" Cara agreed.

Someone knocked on the gate, and Tricia said, "Here they are! Lights! Camera! Action!"

Becky grabbed the sign-in clipboard and ran for the gate. As president of the Twelve Candles Club, she was always first to greet arrivals, then Jess would greet the next, then Tricia, then Cara. That way the kids would feel welcome, and the parents would sign in their child in an organized way.

First, as usual, were Mrs. Davis and her five-year-old twins, Jimjim and Jojo, who had a secret language no one else understood. "Go-go!" they shouted, which was at least in English. They ran to the swings yelling, "Umpty-dumpty-ilt-dumpel-dumel! Umpity-dumpity-lum-lum!"

Car doors slammed one after another out front, and Jess was already on her way to the gate, Tricia right behind her.

Cara hurried to the breezeway, eyeing Jimjim and Jojo, who always shrieked wildly as they swung higher and higher. The backyard was filling, and here came a new mother with her small wide-eyed son.

When Cara's turn came, she barely had a chance to grab the sign-in clipboard from Tricia. *Yipes! Sam Miller!* He looked as innocent as an angel with his blue eyes and blond hair, but he was one kid who could be counted on for t-r-o-u-b-l-e.

"Hello, Mrs. Miller," Cara said, then, "Hello, Sam."

Sam eyed her pirate outfit with disappointment. "Where's your clown suit?" he demanded.

"I . . . ah . . . clowns never give away their identity . . . you know, who they are."

"I want clowns, not pirates!" Sam yelled. "I want clowns . . . clowns . . . CLOWNS!"

His mother said soothingly, "Now, Sam. . . ."

Cara handed her the sign-in paper, which had fill-in spaces for FUNNER'S NAME, AGE, TIME IN, TIME OUT, PARENTS' PHONE, DOCTOR'S NAME/PHONE NUMBER.

Sam was just about to yell again, so Cara said in her best pirate imitation, "Pirates are even better. They're s-c-a-r-y."

Sam eyed her a moment, then tore off to the tree house, which was supposed to be off limits.

"No, Sam, not in the tree house!" Cara called after him. But he was already halfway up the tree.

"Oh, dear," Mrs. Miller said, looking up from the form. "I'm sorry. He does have a mind of his own."

"It's all right for now," Cara answered. "Just so not too many kids get up in it and break the branches down."

Mrs. Miller had no more than finished the sign-in sheet than Becky needed it. Kids poured into the yard faster and faster. Before long, twenty little kids yelled and raced around the backyard. As if that weren't bad enough, the two Coobler boys next door hung their heads over the fence. "Hey, can we come over, Mr. One-eyed Pirate?" they asked Cara in obnoxious tones. "Please? Please?"

"It's just for kids four to seven years old—"

The older boy put on a phoney baby voice. "We're just four and five years old. We want to come visit. We want to come play with the other little boys and girls."

"*Come on!*" she objected. "You're eleven or twelve."

"No, we're not," they baby-voiced again into the growing

racket. "We're just four and five years old. We want to be friends with the kiddies."

Cara tried to pretend that she didn't hear them.

"Hi-ho, me mateys!" Tricia shouted, raising her plastic sword. "If you'll help s-p-r-e-a-d out the m-a-g-i-c c-a-r-p-e-t, we'll set s-a-i-l on our p-i-r-a-t-e g-a-l-l-e-o-n!"

The kids quieted and rushed forward to roll out the raggedy brown carpet. Even Sam Miller climbed down from the tree. But the Coobler boys still hung over the fence, only now they were laughing at them. "Hi-ho, me mateys!" they mimicked over and over, then laughed hilariously.

Tricia raised her plastic sword higher, ignoring them. "Today we're sailing to a p-i-r-a-t-e i-s-l-a-n-d to find the gold we stashed there a few years ago. Everyone ready?" She looked around. "Pull up the ship's g-a-n-g-w-a-y! Up the g-a-n-g-w-a-y so no s-t-o-w-a-w-a-y-s board!"

"Yeah!" the kids yelled, settling on the brown carpet. They pretended to pull in the gangway with her. "Let's go!"

"Pull up the a-n-c-h-o-r. . . !" Tricia called out, hauling up an imaginary anchor. "Up the a-n-c-h-o-r!"

The kids all shouted with her and made believe they were hauling up the anchor with her.

"Now r-a-i-s-e the s-a-i-l!" Tricia commanded, raising an imaginary sail.

Cara stood on the back of the raggedy rug, hoisting the imaginary sail with them. She tried to ignore the Coobler boys laughing like crazy—probably at her for looking so stupid. If they went to junior high next year with them, they'd tell everyone about her playing pirate. They'd be just like Paige, making fun of her.

She turned her attention to Tricia and wished she could do

things as well as Tricia. No matter what Tricia did for the Magic Carpet, she always looked like a real actress, probably because she acted in church skits and Christian Community Theater plays.

"S-e-t s-a-i-l, m-a-t-e-y-s!" Tricia called out to them. "S-e-t s-a-i-l for an exciting a-d-v-e-n-t-u-r-e!"

The first-timer kids peered around. Probably they expected to really take off on the old rug.

"What shall we eat on our s-e-a v-o-y-a-g-e?" Tricia asked. No one seemed really certain, so she sang out a crazy song about "m-u-s-s-e-l-s and m-u-s-s-e-l-s and m-u-s-s-e-l-s and c-l-a-m-s. . . !" Finally, they all sang with her.

The Coobler boys had been making fun of everything, but even they began to quiet.

"And now," Tricia said, pointing at Cara with her sword, "C-a-r-a the P-i-r-a-t-e will tell you 'The Pirate Story.' "

Cara froze. *No. . . !*

The kids all turned to her, and the Coobler boys began to act up again. She couldn't think of one word . . . not one. *Help me*, she prayed. *Help me, God!*

"P-r-e-s-e-n-t-i-n-g 'The P-i-r-a-t-e S-t-o-r-y,' " Tricia announced in her loudest voice.

Cara racked her mind. The story began with three children afloat in the meadow by a swing, but that wouldn't do for these kids. She blurted the first thing that flew to mind, trying to sound dramatic like Tricia and trying to rhyme:

"Twenty-four of us a-f-l-o-a-t
on a p-i-r-a-t-e b-o-a-t,
s-a-i-l-i-n-g a-l-o-n-g on the s-e-a,

s-i-n-g out your names, m-a-t-e-y-s,
so we'll k-n-o-w who's a-b-o-a-r-d. . . .

She pointed at Tricia.

"Aye, aye, . . . Tricia Bennett," she bellowed.

Cara pointed at the Davis twins in the front row.

"Jimjim!" one answered and "Jojo!" yelled the other.

The kids all called out their names as she pointed, and Cara could hardly believe that she—timid old Cara Hernandez—had been able to add to the adventure.

At the end, she pointed behind them at the Coobler boys, who both bellowed, "Doug Coobler!" and "Cody Coobler!"

When they'd finished, she remembered something else. "S-t-e-e-r by the s-t-a-r-s!" she told them, turning an imaginary ship's wheel hard. "S-t-e-e-r by the s-t-a-r-s! Keep your eyes on the M-i-l-k-y W-a-y!"

Watching them all steer their imaginary wheels with her, she couldn't believe it . . . she simply couldn't believe it. Like Tricia, she *could* hold them enthralled.

Suddenly she remembered her prayer. Had God helped her? Had God helped Cara Amelia Hernandez? Could He really make her triumph over shyness?

Then a less exciting thought hit.

If God could really make her triumph over trouble, how could she turn to Him? Forever? If only she could ask someone in her family about it!

CHAPTER

7

June 30

Today at MFK (Morning Fun for Kids), I played back-up pirate and actually made up some of the magic carpet story with Tricia. I couldn't believe I was doing it myself, but the ideas just rolled out of my brain. I did pray, and Tricia says if you trust God, He'll help you with the talent He's given you. I'm still surprised that He'd help me. First, He gave me courage, then He helped me think what to say.

The rest of MFK went fine, too. At least as fine as it ever does with twenty little kids. When it was over, we flung ourselves down on the grass, as usual, and remembered the funny stuff. There were lots of laughs. One: While Jess was showing the kids gymnastics, little Paula Thomas did a somersault and wet her pants! Another: The Coobler boys wouldn't quit watching and, all of a sudden, they both tumbled over the fence and into the yard. Tricia yelled, "Wait till I tell the kids at school that Doug and Cody Coobler came to Morning Fun for Kids—for 'little kids.' " I am almost sure that they won't pester us again!

It was a crazy morning, but we lived through it. In fact, we did all right. At $6 per kid, and subtracting Suzanne and Bryan Bennett and Amanda Hamilton, who come free, we made 17 times $6, which equals $102! Divided by the four of us, we each got $25.50. With that, I've got enough saved up for a new bathing suit—and a new dress for Sunday school, in case I go again, and lots more. I'd rather not ask Mom for a Sunday school outfit since she acted so weird about my going in the first place.

The money is most important for Becky because her dad died a few years ago, and her mom just barely makes enough money to keep them from having to move away. It's important for me, I guess, because Paige has her own money that she inherited. Now I have some of my own, too. Dad says I should start a bank account, but I haven't had time to do it yet. For now, I'm still stuffing the dollar bills into my new shell purse.

Right after MFK, I baby-sat the Davis twins since Mrs. Davis had to go to a meeting at one o'clock, and Becky, who usually sits for them, had to go to the dentist. It was easy since I just had to make peanut butter and jelly sandwiches, and give them milk and cookies for lunch. After that, I read them the same story twice, and they took their nap. They were still sleeping when Mrs. Davis returned. I lucked out! As they say, "Umpty-dumpty-umpel-dum-dum!" Or something that sounds almost like that. At least, they understand.

The worst trouble I had all day wasn't little kids, but with Paige again. When I came home, she was just getting into her car. "Well, Caro-leen-a Hernandez, don't you think you're something?" she yelled so loud the entire neighborhood must have heard her, then she muttered more quietly, "Just because *of you, Brad Tucker doesn't ever want to see me again!"*

When I asked her why, she said it sure was obvious to her as well as to her friends. He didn't care to date a girl with Mexican relatives.

My heart hurt like anything. Finally I got suspicious and asked, "Did he really say that?"

"He didn't have to!" she answered. "Right after their party—and seeing you—he stopped phoning me!"

I was so mad and hurt that I yelled, "Maybe he listened to his Aunt Hattie at the party and saw what you're really like!" (It is probably not what God would want me to say at a time like that, but I don't care.)

She was mad-mad-mad and honked her horn lots of times as she drove away. Sometimes I wonder if she hates me so much because she used to have Mom to herself before Mom married Dad and they had me. She hates Dad, too, I think. Probably it's because we're Hispanic.

Sometimes I wonder if Jess and Tricia and Becky feel a little like that about me, too? Worst of all, I'm all mixed up about it myself. I'm going to try to remember that God made every person different and special, like Bear said Sunday. I'll try to remember that means me!

"This meeting will now come to order," Becky announced. She sat backwards on Jess's white wooden desk chair and pounded her hand on the top of the back rest.

Cara settled on a twin bed with her secretary's notebook and tried hard to forget about Paige's hatred, not that it was the least bit easy.

One thing, she felt more at ease in Jess's room than in any of the other TCC girls' bedrooms. Probably because they'd met there every weekday from four-thirty to five-thirty ever since the club started almost one month ago. And maybe because Jess's bedroom looked more like a gym.

Actually, it'd been a three-car garage, now remodeled into a huge white room with a high-beamed ceiling and louvered blinds on the windows. Besides white twin beds, a chest of drawers and matching desk, there were floor mats, parallel bars, a small trampoline, a gymnast's beam, a ballet *barre* in front of a huge mirror, and enormous posters on the walls of Olympic gymnasts like Mary Lou Retton, Nadia Comaneci, and Julianne McNamara.

Also Jess had an antique trunk she inherited from Elspeth and Oakley McColl who'd come to California to start a church during the gold rush almost 150 years ago. Better to think about that than about Paige's hatred.

As they finally came "to order," Becky asked, "Will the secretary please read the minutes?"

Cara wished she didn't have to read about the last meeting since it'd been the night of the *Moonstreams* video disaster. She tried to forget that, too, and made herself read from her secretary's notebook in a businesslike manner.

"The last meeting of the Twelve Candles Club was on Friday, June 27, at Cara Hernandez's house. Old business. We discussed the Tuckers' outdoor buffet and the Saturday morning car-washing list of fifteen regulars. We had one baby-sitting job cancelled and switched the Terhunes' Saturday afternoon housecleaning to Monday afternoon because of the Tuckers' party on Saturday.

"The treasurer's report showed $24.55 and no bills. President Becky Hamilton suggested that we pay part of Jess McColl's phone bill every month since we use her phone for the club. Jess said that her father was glad to pay for it since her working for the club saved him lots of money. No new business. Respectfully submitted, Cara Amelia Hernandez, Secretary."

"Thank you," Becky said in her formal voice. "Any additions or corrections?"

Not surprisingly, Jess hopped onto her trampoline and answered between bounces. "Only that we've come a long way . . . from that first meeting . . . when Becky said she . . . didn't know how . . . to conduct a meeting!"

Becky grinned, but stuck to business. "Does anyone move that the minutes of the meeting of June 27 be approved as read?"

"I so move," Tricia said.

"I second the motion," Jess put in, still bouncing.

"It has been moved and seconded that the minutes of the meeting of June 27 be accepted as read. Is there any discussion?"

Cara hoped not, especially not discussion about *Moonstreams*, and was glad to see there was none.

"The minutes of the meeting of June 27 are accepted as read," Becky announced. "May we now have the treasurer's report from Tricia Bennett?"

Tricia straightened her back and read in a comical voice, "Ze treasurer reports still $24.55 in ze treasury, and no new bills for ze TCC club to pay."

Becky rolled her eyes. "Any old business?"

Cara raised a hand. "I saw Mrs. Terhune out by her mailbox. She only wants us to clean every other Saturday afternoon now that she's up and around and their new baby sleeps more."

Tricia jumped up and headed for the green chalkboard over

Jess's desk. "I write it down on ze chalkboard so ve don't forget it."

"Come on, Tricia!" Becky protested. "What's with the German accent?"

"Just practicing in case I get a German part someday," Tricia answered. She wrote in *Terhune* for the Saturday after next. At first, it'd been Cara's job to chalk up the information, but they'd found she had enough to do with writing down the minutes. So Tricia was now treasurer and the official chalkboard person.

The phone rang and Becky picked it up. "Twelve Candles Club. Oh yes, Mrs. Llewellyn. Yes, we'll be there to clean again Thursday. We already have it up on the board." She listened, rolling her eyes again. "A luncheon Saturday after next? How many of us would you need? Two? Just a moment while I ask." She put her hand over the phone's mouthpiece since Mrs. Llewellyn always refused to wait for call-backs.

"Two to set the tables and help serve at a luncheon for twelve at Mrs. L's," Becky explained. "We'll have to work around all of the car washing. Who wants to work the luncheon?"

Cara shook her head. "Not me unless there's no one else. I'd rather wash cars." Mrs. L might pay more, but washing cars was lots easier than serving twelve ladies who'd probably watch your every move. The Tuckers' party had been enough of that for a long while.

"Me too," Jess put in, still bouncing on the trampoline. "I'd rather . . . wash cars."

Tricia raised a hand. "I'll work for Mrs. L."

"I will too," Becky said.

Tricia chalked up:

Saturday, July 12
Mrs. L luncheon
Becky & Tricia

Becky said into the phone, "Tricia and I are available, Mrs. Llewellyn. What time?" She listened for a moment. "Eleven until three."

Tricia gave a nod and added *11 to 3* on the chalkboard.

"Thank you, Mrs. Llewelleyn. We'll wear our white skirts and blouses unless you have something else in mind. . . .What do we have? Well, the western outfits you gave us, clown suits, and two pirate outfits."

Cara and Tricia muffled their giggles. You never knew what Mrs. L had planned.

"Fine," Becky replied. "White skirts and blouses. We'll be there. You can count on us."

She'd no more than hung up than the phone rang again. A clown birthday party for a friend of the Davis twins. A minute later, a window-washing job at the Herringtons', who'd just returned from a vacation in Australia.

After that came five baby-sitting phone calls, and Cara took one with the Marshalls since they only had a girl, and she was already eight years old.

The next time Becky picked up the phone, she listened, then said, "Just one moment." She put her hand over the mouthpiece and turned to Cara. "For 'Caro-leen-a' Hernandez. It sounds like Paige."

Cara rolled her eyes and took the phone. "Hello?"

"*Buenas tardes*, Caro-leen-a Hernandez," Paige answered. "Your mama wants you home now to start dinner."

Cara bristled at her sister's nasty tone. "I'm not coming

home until 5:30, as usual," she told her. "We're taking phone calls now. Why don't *you* start dinner?"

"Your mama will not be very happy to hear you refused," Paige answered.

"She knows we take phone calls now!"

"Oh, really. . . ? Well, it's your funeral, *Señorita!*" Paige yelled, and the phone clicked in Cara's ear.

"What's wrong?" Tricia asked.

Cara grimaced. "Nothing." She decided not to go home until after 5:30, as usual. Mom and Dad knew she was always here at Jess's taking TCC phone calls now. And they were glad she was working.

Jess hopped off the trampoline. "Something is wrong, Cara. You want to tell us?"

She hesitated, then asked, "Does it make any difference to you that I'm part Mexican?"

"What?! Cara—what are you talking about?" Jess demanded.

"Well, Paige is always—"

"Oh, brother!" Tricia put in. "Or should I say, sister! Paige is out to get you—any way she can!"

"What do you mean?" Cara asked.

"Cara," Becky said, "you're our friend. Nothing more, and nothing less. We don't think much at all about what nationality you are. You're just our friend Cara, that's all."

"Oh, I didn't know . . . that is, I. . . ."

"Your sister's just out to make you mad."

"So what else is new?" Jess asked.

"Just remember, ve are your friends," Tricia announced firmly. "Ve are your friends."

"Thanks," she told them, grateful. But it wasn't too much

later that she began to wonder: Did they sometimes do a Hispanic accent and laugh at her, too?

After the meeting ended, she trudged across the street, dreading what kind of trouble Paige might have waiting for her. Her sister's red Thunderbird stood in the driveway. Probably she and her snobby friends were still blaming her for Brad Tucker not calling.

Cara headed around to the backyard, as usual, and got the hidden key from under one of the red clay flowerpots. She was about to poke it into the back doorknob when Paige pulled open the door.

She beamed her wide cheerleader smile. "Well, if it isn't the working girl! Why didn't you just knock on the door so I could let you in?"

Cara shrugged. "Didn't know you'd be in the kitchen." Besides, it was best not to ask Paige to do anything because she'd be sure to yell, *"Whose slave do you think I am?"* On top of that, she didn't want to be blamed again for Paige losing Brad Tucker.

Paige looked strangely sweet and innocent in an old white sundress. "You know," she said, "it might be a good idea for us to be friends."

"Friends?!" Cara repeated. "Us?" Her mind flashed back to her sister tripping her at the Tuckers' party, making her spill the salsa on Mrs. Tucker's head.

"Why not?" Paige asked, still smiling. "We're only half sisters anyhow. Since that hasn't worked out so well, maybe we could try to be friends. We used to be more friendly."

Cara looked at her suspiciously. From the corner of her

eye, she saw even Angora watching Paige doubtfully from a dining room chair.

"Come on in," Paige said. "I've already set the table and made the salad. I thought maybe we could bake some cookies or something for dessert. There's a roll of chocolate chip cookie dough in the fridge."

Cara felt even more suspicious. Still, maybe Paige meant it. Maybe Brad Tucker's rejection made her realize how she usually acted. "All right," Cara answered slowly.

"I'll get out the cookie sheets and turn on the oven," her sister added. "I've already read the directions. We have to bake the enchilada casserole Mom made this morning, too."

Cara could only stare. Finally she asked, "Did you call Mom and tell her I couldn't make the salad and set the table because of the club meeting?"

"Why should I?" Paige asked innocently.

Cara shrugged. After a moment, she managed, "Thanks for doing it for me."

"Sure," Paige said. "I used the napkin rings. Doesn't the table look nice?"

Cara glanced at the table in their dining area. Paige had even used the peach tablecloth instead of their usual place mats. What was going on with her? What could have changed since her nasty phone call not even an hour ago? It was sure nice to have Paige act pleasant, but it had been such a long time since she hadn't been nasty that this was totally u-n-b-e-l-i-e-v-a-b-l-e.

CHAPTER

8

When Mom and Dad stepped through the front door, soft music swirled through the house, and the aroma of enchilada casserole mingled with the smell of freshly baked chocolate chip cookies. If Cara weren't so suspicious of Paige, she might have enjoyed it more.

"Ummmm . . . smells good," Mom said, surprised.

Paige smiled. "Cara and I did it together."

Mom's blue-gray eyes sparkled, making her look pretty in her blue-gray pant suit. "Well, I am impressed! I can't believe you actually worked together to make dinner. Doesn't it make a wonderful difference if you two act like sisters should?"

Paige smiled sweetly, and Cara tried not to look dubious. She managed a hopeful "Yes." She darted a glance at her father, whose brown eyes viewed Paige warily, too.

"I'm glad to see it," he said in a skeptical voice. "I hope it continues. It would certainly make life more pleasant if we acted like a real family."

Mom shot him a warning look.

"Come along," Paige urged. "Sit down and have dinner. Cara and I will serve. Cara picked the daisies for the table. Aren't they pretty?"

"Very nice," Mom answered. "I've been so busy, I'd forgotten that we still had daisies growing in the yard."

Paige turned, the skirt of her white sundress swirling. "Come on, Cara, let's get dinner on the table."

Cara followed her into the kitchen. She half expected Paige to change back to her nasty old self any moment, but she either wanted to be different or was a good actress.

"Why don't you toss the salad," her sister suggested most pleasantly. "I'll carry in the casserole so you don't burn yourself."

Cara headed for the refrigerator, still not quite believing what was happening. "Thanks."

Maybe Paige was going to ask Mom and Dad for something big, Cara thought. But what? She already had a car and her closet was stuffed with clothes. Maybe she wanted to go to Hawaii or Europe with her rich friends. Yep, that must be what she was up to.

All through dinner, Cara waited to hear a humongous request, but nothing happened. Instead, Paige was perfect, a-b-s-o-l-u-t-e-l-y p-e-r-f-e-c-t.

When they finished, Mom said, "This is one of the nicest dinners we've had together in ages. Thank you, girls, for being so considerate."

Paige raised her brows thoughtfully. "We should always be like this," she said. "Always, always."

Mom sat back in her chair with a contented smile. "We won't argue with that."

Cara and her father didn't say anything. Now Paige would ask for whatever it was, Cara thought. N-o-w was the moment she would strike.

Instead, Paige hopped up from her chair and began to clear the table. "Sit, everyone," she told them. "I'll bring in the cookies."

Cara still couldn't believe it. But while her parents were in a good mood, it seemed a good time to mention something herself. "Ummm . . . would it be all right if I go to the church beach party with Tricia, Becky, and Jess tomorrow?" She rushed on. "It's from four until seven, so we'd be home way before dark."

Mom glanced at Dad, and he nodded.

"Sounds fine, as long as there are adults with you," Mom answered, eyeing her thoughtfully.

"Bear . . . I mean the minister will be there," Cara assured her, "and probably others."

"Bear?" Mom repeated.

Cara nodded. "That's what everyone calls him. He even looks a little like one . . . you know, a smiley bear."

"What a name for a minister!" Mom remarked. "Things have surely changed since my day."

"But no dates," her father said in his firmest voice. "You hear me? No dates."

"Who *me*? Are you kidding?"

She'd asked it with such amazement that they all smiled. She added, "The only guys who notice me and the other TCC girls are those Coobler boys, and they're stupid kids. They fell right over the Bennetts' fence when they were laughing at Morning Fun for Kids this morning! It's a wonder they didn't crack their heads!" Mom and Dad both laughed and just remembering it made her laugh with them.

Tuesday morning at eight-thirty, Jess was waiting out in front on her bike. "We're off!" she announced as Cara rode out of the garage on her bike.

"Way off!" Cara answered happily. She was the first one in her family out this morning. The Flicks van still stood in the driveway, and Mom's old Honda was in the garage, as was Paige's Thunderbird.

It was a little foggy, which made the neighborhood look mysterious as they pedaled down La Crescenta side by side. Here and there, neighbors set out in their cars for work, and most of the kids were still inside their houses. The air was cool, and Cara was glad she'd worn her jeans.

After a while, she asked, "Are you going to the church beach party?"

"Phooey! I forgot to ask," Jess admitted.

"I did last night at dinner. And, would you believe, I can!" Cara told her. "I was almost afraid to ask, but Paige was so nice for a change that everything was perfect."

"Paige was *nice*?" Jess asked. "Are you talking about *Paige Larson*?"

Cara nodded. "I can't figure it out. I thought for sure that she was going to ask my parents for something totally outrageous, but she didn't."

"Wonder what she's up to," Jess said.

"That's what worries me."

Cara thought about what she had written in her journal that morning: *Tricia says she and Becky have been praying for Paige and me. If Paige really does stay nice like this, I will very definitely believe in miracles!*

They coasted to a stop between Tricia's and Becky's houses to wait for them. Jess called out, "Come on, you guys, we're waiting!"

A second later, Becky walked her bike out from her garage. "I have to close the garage door."

Tricia rode out of her garage. "Why is the sky high?" she asked dramatically. "What skuds the clouds overhead? Who makes the lightning flash? Are the angels dancing on pinheads?"

"Search me," Jess answered.

"Sounds like a poet in action," Cara said.

"Oh," Jess answered, then shook her head. "Well, the sky and clouds and lightning are very small stuff compared to something else. The real question is what's making Paige act nice to Cara?"

"Paige nice?" Tricia asked, waiting on her bike beside them.

Becky hopped on her bike and coasted down her driveway. "Paige acting nice?" she echoed.

"It's the mystery of the ages," Jess told them. "We figure something's up."

"Maybe God's been speaking to her," Tricia put in as they set out riding along La Crescenta.

"You mean that would change her?" Cara asked.

"Sure," Becky answered. "Jesus can change a person all the way around. He can take bad and make it good."

"Paige didn't say anything about that," Cara said. "She doesn't even think much of my going to Sunday school or a church beach party."

"Then it's the mystery of the ages, all right," Tricia agreed. "Whoa! That means you're going to the beach party today with us!"

"I am!"

"All right!" Tricia and Becky called out.

"I still have to ask," Jess said, "but I bet I can. I hope the sun comes out."

They rode to Ocean Boulevard and crossed at the stoplights to head west toward the ocean. Morning traffic was too heavy for talking as they rode along in the bike lane.

Even after they arrived at the O'Lones' big Spanish house and began cleaning, the question was still on their minds. Every once in a while one of them would call out over the roar of the vacuum, "What's making Paige Larson change?"

Cara truly wished she knew. She had a sinking feeling that whatever it was might not be good.

When they returned home at noon after working, the sun was finally coming out. Cara parked her bike in the garage, and, not surprisingly, found the cars and the Flicks van gone.

What was surprising was a loud "Meow!"

"Angora! What are you doing outside?"

She opened the back door to let their cat in, then headed through the quiet house toward her room to put away her morning's earnings. Angora had bounded in and was settling on the window seat, and Cara went straight to the closet.

Something's strange, she thought. The closet seemed even messier than usual; she'd have to straighten up the purses, bookbag, and other stuff on the top shelf. But first, after lunch, she had to ride her bike down to the Santa Rosita Mall to buy a new swimsuit for the beach party. She hoped they would have something m-o-d-e-s-t.

She got down her white seashell purse and opened it.

Empty!

It was empty!

Every bit of her money was gone!

She stood staring into the empty purse, feeling she must be stuck in a nightmare. Who could have taken her money?

A thought hit. Maybe Mom or Dad borrowed it. Still holding her purse, she ran from her room and down the hallway for the kitchen phone. Sure, they'd borrowed it, that's all. They were driving to Los Angeles and probably didn't have time to go to the bank. They knew she kept her money in the closet; that's why Dad kept telling her to open a bank account.

She dialed the Flicks number and was relieved to hear her father answer.

"It's Cara. Did you borrow the money from my purse in my closet, Dad?"

"No," he answered. "Why?"

"It's all gone!" she cried out. "Every bit of it!"

"Let me ask your mother."

He came back on the phone a second later. "She didn't borrow it, either. Look around and see if there's any sign of a burglar. Are the TV and VCR still there? Are the rooms messed up, or the garage? Is there anyone in the backyard?"

Cara craned her neck around the archway to look into the living room. "The TV and VCR are still there. And the house isn't messed up. Only my closet was a little. I just came home through the backyard, and no one was there. Nothing was wrong in the garage, either."

"Is Paige there?" he asked in an odd voice.

"No, I'm . . . I'm alone," she answered shakily. "And, you know what? Angora was outside in the backyard, waiting to get in. You know how she hates to be outside."

"I'll be there in a few minutes," he said. "Your mother will have to hold the fort here. I don't think we want to call the police . . . not now. Just stay calm. And wait outside by the front door, just in case. See you in a few minutes."

Cara hung up, straining her ears as she hurried through the house to the front door, but everything was quiet. Only birds twittered in the trees outside the windows. No one seemed to be in the garage, either. She sat down on the front steps, trying to be very quiet.

Finally, Dad drove up in the van and jumped out. "You all right, *amiga*?" he asked.

She nodded and smiled a little, since he only called her *amiga* when they were alone and he meant to show how much he really loved her.

"I was thinking," he said, "maybe Paige borrowed your money until she could get out to the bank. That's probably it. You know what a hurry she's always in. But let's have a thorough look around."

Cara followed him through the living room, dining area, and kitchen, then through the hallway to check the bath and the three bedrooms. One thing about a small house, it was fast to inspect, even the closets. In her room, the shutters were closed, but sunshine filtering through the slats gave lots of light, enough for Angora to enjoy the window seat again.

Her father checked out her closet shelf and the empty purse, then shook his head. "The only answer is that Paige must have borrowed it."

"You'd think she'd ask me!"

"You'd think so," Dad agreed with a small frown. "Paige never does what you expect. We need to talk to her before we take any other action."

He gave her his beautiful smile, the one that went all the way to his brown eyes. "Come on, let's make some sandwiches for lunch. Don't worry, we'll get to the bottom of this."

Cara still felt shaken, but having her father around helped a lot. They headed for the kitchen and began to make lunch-meat and cheese sandwiches with tomato slices.

When they sat down at the white-tiled counter, he said, "Don't forget, today your mother and I drive to Los Angeles to see about adding a new store there. We should have left an hour ago, so we won't be back until late."

"I remembered," Cara said. "I was afraid that I'd missed you already."

"Paige promised to be around this afternoon, so you won't be alone," he told her.

After he left, she had to feed Angora, empty the dishwasher, and take out the garbage. Then she remembered to take the garbage cans out front. Finally she returned to her room. *A new bathing suit!* She'd forgotten all about needing one for the beach party at four o'clock—and now she had no money to buy it!

She rushed back to the phone and called Flicks.

"Your parents just left," the part-time man said.

"Uffffffff!" Cara answered. "Thanks anyhow."

She went back to her room and dug out her faded yellow swimsuit. It looked pretty bad.

She'd just pulled it on when she heard Paige drive up, squealing her tires into the driveway. Cara opened a shutter to look out her window. It was Paige, all right. Paige saw her through the window and gave a friendly wave.

She'd never get used to the new Paige, Cara decided as she made her way to the front door. At least her sister's red shorts and scoop-necked Tee looked familiar.

As Paige stepped in, Cara asked, "Did you borrow my

money? Did you take it from my purse?"

Paige's blue eyes flashed with uncertainty, then she smiled her bright cheerleader smile. "Who me? Why would I take your money?"

"I . . . I just thought maybe you couldn't get to the bank, or something."

Paige shook her head, her eyes full of innocence and her tousled hair tumbling over her shoulders. "Not me. Whew, what are you doing in that ugly swimsuit?"

Cara looked down at herself. "It's my only one. My money's all disappeared, and I need a swimsuit for the beach party." She glanced at the whirligig clock on the mantel. It was almost two-thirty. "We leave in an hour. Could I borrow some money from you so I can buy a swimsuit on the way?"

Paige's eyes widened. "I don't have any . . . I mean. . . ." She let her words trail off and pressed her lips together nervously.

"You don't have any?!" Cara repeated.

Paige nodded, still biting her lips.

"You took it!" Cara shouted. "You took my money! That's why you're acting so nice!"

"I did not!" Paige retorted and pushed her way past.

"Paige Larson, give me my money back!" Cara demanded. She rushed behind her sister toward her room. Furious, she added, "If you don't, I'm going to call the police."

Paige stopped and turned in her room's doorway. "*Come on!*" she huffed. "You can't think I'd actually steal your money?"

Cara nodded. "I wouldn't be surprised. I bet that's why you suddenly started acting so sugary-sweet yesterday."

Paige straightened up angrily. "Let's go look in your room to see if it's really missing."

Cara followed her into her own room.

"Where was it?" Paige asked.

Cara marched around her and flung open the closet doors. She took down the white seashell purse and opened it. "Here, and it's empty! As if you didn't know!"

"Don't yell at me! Let's look around and see if someone got in." She went to the shutters over the window seat, making Angora jump down and whiz away like a white streak through the room for the hallway. Opening the shutters on the right, Paige exclaimed, "Look! Your screen's torn off!" She glanced down. "It's down there behind the bushes! Besides that, your window wasn't even locked! And you're accusing me—"

"How'd you happen to go right to that side of the window and see it?" Cara demanded. "I looked out before and didn't even notice the screen was off."

"Anyone knows burglars come in through windows," her sister answered. "You should have looked carefully before accusing me."

"I don't believe you!"

"I don't care!" Paige shouted back. "Look, even after you've accused me of . . . of stealing, I'm willing to help. I've got old bikinis that don't fit me anymore. I'll let you wear my very favorite old one," she said, and started down the hall toward her room.

"We're supposed to wear *modest* swimsuits," Cara said, following her. "It's a church beach party."

"*Come on!*" Paige repeated. "What have they got against bikinis? Everyone wears them! Look, you can wear one of mine and worry about your money later." She pulled a red and white polka-dot bikini from her drawer.

Cara drew a miserable breath. What if Paige was telling the truth? After all, the screen was down, and it was hard to believe that her sister would go outside in the bushes to pull it off. Besides, Mom and Dad were gone now, so she couldn't get money from them. It was true, too, that most girls wore bikinis.

"All right," she said, taking the bikini. "I'll wear it, but I'll keep my shorts and top on."

"You'd think I wasn't doing you a favor," Paige answered, indignant.

Cara shot back a bitter, "Thanks a lot," and returned to her room. She'd no more than put the bikini on and pulled her top and shorts over it, than the doorbell rang.

"I'll get it," Paige called out.

"Flowers for Cara Hernandez," a man said.

"For Cara?!" Paige repeated.

Puzzled, Cara rushed to the front door herself.

Paige was just closing the door, and she held a brass pot filled with glorious peach-colored azaleas.

"For me?" Cara asked.

"That's what he said," Paige replied with disbelief. "And it says Cara Hernandez on the florist's envelope."

Cara accepted the flowers from her, not quite believing someone had sent her flowers. She carried them to the glass-topped coffee table in the living room. Taking the envelope out of the azaleas, she opened it and read, *With gratefulness for jumping in when you were needed. Brad Tucker and family.*

Paige had read it over her shoulder, and she let out a furious "Well! I hope you're satisfied! You've driven my boyfriend away from me, and now he's treating you like a princess, just like your stupid Mexican father always does." Her eyes were narrowed, and she was breathing heavily. "You're just Daddy's Little Girl, aren't you? Well, I've gotten along fine without a father, but I won't let you steal my boyfriend away from me."

To Cara's amazement, she saw tears in Paige's eyes.

"It's not fair!" Paige yelled. "I've worked hard to win Brad Tucker. He's mine, and I won't let you have him!"

Paige stood there, glaring at her, and Cara wasn't sure what to do. Bewildered, she said quite honestly, "Paige, I'm not interested in your boyfriend. What would I want with a college boy, anyway? If you were just a little nicer person, maybe he'd still be interested in you—"

"There's nothing wrong with *me*," Paige shouted. "NOTHING! But there sure is something wrong with you. The only way you can attract a boy is by dragging him through the water by the hair. HUH! Well, I don't need you, and I don't need your stupid father, either." And with that, she stomped out of the room.

Cara sighed. Just when she thought things were getting better between her and Paige, this had to happen.

Best to put the flowers in her bedroom so her sister wouldn't be reminded, Cara decided. It was nice of Brad—or maybe his parents—to send flowers, but it didn't help the least bit with her missing money!

Worst of all, Paige was furious.

CHAPTER

9

Cara debated going to the beach party. She sure wasn't in a party mood. But she couldn't stay around the house, either, not with Paige still there and her parents gone. Probably it'd be better to go.

What was the matter with Paige, anyway? she thought as she rode her bike down the driveway. Why would Paige say she was stealing Brad? Probably it'd just popped from her mouth because she was mad. Anyhow, Cara felt sure her half sister was right about one thing: Cara Hernandez was so shy and such a klutz that she'd never attract any boys . . . even when she was old enough to date.

Oh, I just hate my life! she thought. *Everything I do turns out wrong! I've tried to act like a Christian, but lots of good it's done me. My money's all gone, my sister hates me more than ever, and—as usual—my parents are too busy to stay home with me when there's trouble. Nothing good ever happens to me. Nothing! Nothing! Nothing!*

At three-thirty, Cara and Jess coasted their bikes to a stop in front of Tricia's and Becky's houses. Still shaky after the scene with Paige, and being robbed, Cara decided that the kids at the beach party probably wouldn't like her, either.

"We're waiting!" Jess shouted at Tricia's and Becky's houses. "Hurry it up before the traffic gets too heavy on Ocean Avenue!"

Voices called back from both houses, so the two of them stood straddling their bikes to wait. "Got your bathing suit on under your shorts and Tee?" Jess asked.

Cara nodded. And that was exactly where Paige's skimpy red bathing suit would stay—under her white shorts and yellow polka-dotted shirt.

"Me too," Jess said. "I'm not riding down Ocean Avenue in a bathing suit and have all kinds of jokers and weirdos honking at me. Remember when we rode across in our clown suits on the way to the Davis twins' birthday party?"

"Uh huh," Cara answered and looked away. It didn't even seem funny anymore. Instead, she felt dead inside. D-e-a-d.

"Cara, something's wrong with you," Jess said, concerned. "What's happened?"

Cara thought it over, then decided maybe Jess could help. "I . . . I've got to tell you something. When . . . when I came home at noon, all my money from working this summer was . . . gone."

"G-o-n-e-!" Jess echoed as only she could.

Cara nodded. "I kept it in my white seashell purse in my closet. At first, I thought my parents borrowed it, but they didn't. I spent the whole last hour searching my room over and over—"

"Paige took it!" Jess said. "I'll bet you anything in the world that she did."

"But she didn't act like she did," Cara answered. "And then, on top of everything, Brad Tucker sent me flowers for saving him in the pool."

"You're kidding!"

Cara shook her head.

"I can imagine Paige boiling when she saw that!"

"She was."

"But it's nothing compared to your money being gone. Think how hard we've worked—"

Just then, Tricia and Becky rode their bikes out. "We're off!" Tricia yelled.

"*Off* is right!" Jess returned. "Someone stole all of Cara's money from her closet!"

"Stole it?" Becky and Tricia asked, coasting their bikes to a stop.

"Who?" Becky asked.

"I bet Paige did it," Jess put in.

"Why would Paige do it?" Becky asked. "She inherited all of that money from her Grandmother Larson."

Cara decided not to tell them that Paige had hinted she'd already used up her money. "Let's ride. I don't want to think about it anymore. It'll spoil the whole afternoon. Maybe Dad will call the police tomorrow. He and Mom are in L.A. now."

"There's no sense in talking about it anyhow," Tricia said, "not when we can pray. Let's bow our heads and ask God to help Cara." She paused and Cara decided she'd better bow her head with them.

"Heavenly Father," Tricia began, "You've heard all of this, about how Cara's money is missing. You know how hard she worked to earn it, and we pray that You'll get the money returned, and that You'll use all of this trouble in a miraculous way to Your glory. We pray in the precious and powerful name of Jesus. Amen."

"Amen," Becky added.

Cara and Jess didn't say anything.

They rode off up La Crescenta, their beach towels under the bikes' back racks. Jess led the way, then Tricia behind her, then Becky and Cara.

One thing about Tricia's prayer, Cara decided, it made you feel better to think that God might take care of things. Anyhow, she wouldn't think about her problems again today if she could help it.

Once they were pedaling along in the bike lane on Ocean Avenue, the nearby lane of cars and trucks kept her mind plenty busy. Probably Tricia and Becky had already prayed for their safety. Maybe their mothers, too.

A long time later, they rode across the Pacific Coast Highway and into the beach parking lot. Jess led the way straight to the bike racks, where they climbed off and could see a great view of the shimmering blue Pacific Ocean.

"There they are!" Tricia exclaimed, glancing at their group down at the beach. "There, by the big red and white umbrella over the ice chests, bags, and other stuff. Looks like lots of kids came. Probably mostly junior highers. They've already set up a volleyball net."

"They'll probably ignore us," Becky said. "They'll say we're not even teenagers."

"Maybe they won't," Tricia answered. "They're supposed to be Christians, although some might have brought other friends. I'll bet Bear told the older kids to welcome us."

Cara hoped so. There were already twenty or more kids. She felt like turning around and running, but she parked her bike in the bike rack, grabbed her beach towel, and followed her friends down the concrete ramp to the beach.

About halfway down, the rumble of cars and trucks on the highway had faded and was replaced by the muffled roar of the ocean. Overhead, the sun shone brightly, and the ocean sparkled a silvery blue as far as she could see. Cara loved the smell of the salt air and the thunder of waves rolling in from far away across the Pacific . . . maybe from Japan or Australia, or who knew where?

At the bottom of the ramp, she pulled off her tennies with the others, then they stepped out onto the sand. "Yikes! It's hot!" Cara yelped as it burned her feet.

"You know it!" Tricia said, running ahead.

"Hey!" Bear yelled, "here's Tricia and Becky! We saved you some sand, but didn't save any food for you, cuz we know you're always on a diet. So we ate it all before you came."

"Thanks a lot!" Tricia and Becky answered, laughing.

As they ran across the hot sand, Cara noticed that Bear looked just as much like a friendly Teddy Bear in his blue swim trunks and a Tee that said, *LOOK TO GOD FOR ALL THE ANSWERS!* The O's in the word "LOOK" were eyes glancing upward, topped with long eyelashes.

The kids lounging on beach towels smiled at them, nice and friendly. Maybe being at the beach with them would turn an awful day into something better.

The girls all wore one-piece swimsuits, though. V-e-r-y m-o-d-e-s-t. Between the shock of her missing money and receiving flowers from Brad Tucker, she hadn't had time to worry about wearing Paige's old bikini. Probably she'd just keep her shorts and Tee on.

"Let's sit here, near the ice chests," Tricia said, making Bear and some of the older kids laugh. "So we're a little hungry," she added, grinning.

"Tricia Bennett's mother doesn't raise dumb kids," Bear joked. "Now let's introduce all four of you. Everyone, this is Tricia Bennett, Becky Hamilton . . . and, oh-oh, I remember you other two, but I'm afraid I don't remember your names."

"Jess McColl," Jess said. "We just came last Sunday."

"Cara Hernandez," Cara added, not surprised that nobody remembered her. She was just a nobody anyhow. She wondered, though, how the kids would react to her Hispanic name, but they were just smiling or giving them a friendly wave.

"Whew!" Bear said. "My memory is going. Must be all this sun. Welcome! Come pull up a piece of sand."

They laughed and threw out their beach towels to spread them, since their feet were still burning on the sand.

Cara hopped onto her salmon-colored beach towel between Jess and Becky, quickly sitting down to let the bottoms of her feet cool off. She noticed that Becky had settled on one side of them, and Tricia on the other. Probably to make them feel surrounded by friends.

The first thing the others did was peel off their shorts and tops from over their swimsuits. Tricia's and Becky's were modest, all right, but pretty. Tricia's suit had a colorful "stained glass" top, a shocking pink middle, and a black bottom. Becky's was made of color wraps—wide strips of light blue, light green, and royal blue—that looked perfect on her lanky body. And Jess's, though a two-piece, was tan and meant for serious swimming, not showing off.

Of all of them, Cara realized with a shock, her figure was filling out the most.

"Aren't you going to take off your shorts and shirt?" Becky asked Cara.

Cara shook her head. "Maybe later. Right now, I want my feet to cool off."

"Do you have a new swimsuit?" Jess asked.

Cara almost said, "New for me," but stopped herself and just nodded as she looked out at the ocean.

"Well, let's see it," Tricia urged.

"Come on, why are you bugging me?" Cara answered, almost exploding. She lowered her voice. "Maybe I feel weird about being in a bathing suit in front of these kids. Did you ever think of that?"

"Not me," Tricia answered, then got up. "I'll get us some chips and dip. Becky, come get Cokes."

Cara stared out at the waves rolling in across the beach. She'd really like to swim, but she couldn't very well do so with her shorts and shirt over her swimsuit. She'd just have to sit there while everybody else had a good time.

Becky brought the Cokes, and Tricia returned and put paper plates with mounds of chips and dips on Cara's and Jess's towels near their feet. The chips and onion and bean dips tasted good, and they all reached for them over and over, eating as if they hadn't seen food in weeks.

After a while, the volleyball players finished their game and headed for the chips and dips themselves. "Hey," one of the guys said, "let's cool off with a swim."

"Good idea," Tricia said, getting up. "I am definitely ready for one."

"Me too," Becky answered, rising to her feet.

And Jess was already up, too. "Last one in is a minnow!" she declared, running across the sand with them.

Cara watched them run into the ocean. They'd already forgotten all about her, she thought.

Bear and most of the other kids had gone in for a swim, too. As she sat there alone on her beach towel, the sun beat down on her. She watched Jess, Tricia, and Becky diving into the waves, then bodysurfing toward shore. When their waves slowed near the beach, they'd get to their feet and go out for another good wave. Just like she would if she could join them.

As she watched, her skin became warmer and warmer, and her shorts and T-shirt felt damp. If only she could fling herself into the ocean, too. Maybe wearing her old swimsuit would have been better than being stuck on the beach. *Dummo Cara.*

She looked around. All kinds of beach-goers surrounded them—some older, and some with little kids, but none sat close by. Just a few minutes ago, three older guys had settled to her right. They were all lounging on their beach towels now, except one who reached into their ice chest. To her amazement, they pulled out cans of beer—which were definitely n-o-t allowed on the beach.

One of them caught her staring. "Hey, ba-bee, you wanna have a beer with us?" He was muscular like Bear, but darker and very handsome.

Cara shook her head and turned away fast.

"Come on, ba-bee, be friendly," he said.

She looked over at the Sunday school group's volleyball players who hadn't gone in swimming yet. They were too far away to notice the guy talking to her.

She darted a glance back at him.

"Hey," he called, "you're really somethin'. I like girls with dark hair like yours. See, I've got dark hair, too. I bet you've got brown eyes. I bet anythin' you got brown eyes."

She shot a drop-dead look at him and turned away, but he only said, "See, didn't I tell ya? Brown eyes. Maybe I'll sing that song for you, 'My Brown-eyed Girl.' "

Cara pressed her lips together, a little annoyed and a little flattered.

"Come on, Rolf, forget it!" one of the other guys protested. "She's a little kid. She's probably still in junior high."

"Big deal," Rolf answered him. "I think she is one v-e-r-y c-u-t-e ba-bee."

Cara pretended not to hear, but she didn't mind knowing they thought she looked nice. It was the first time she'd heard anything at all like that from any guy.

"Hey, Brown Eyes," Rolf called to her. "You there all by yourself? Maybe we could come sit with you."

Cara swallowed. What would Bear and the rest of them think if they came back and found her sitting with these beer-drinking guys? Maybe she should tell them she was with a Sunday school group to keep them away. Maybe she should tell them to leave her alone.

"Come on," Rolf said, "let's take our beers and go sit with Miss Brown Eyes."

Cara glanced at the last of the volleyball players. They were running out into the water now, too. When she looked at the older guys, they were actually starting to move their towels and ice chest over by her.

"Go away!" she said. "I'm here . . . with friends."

"Friends?" Rolf echoed. "They're not such good friends, leavin' you here alone. If I had a cute friend like you, I'd sure stay nearby," he said, walking toward her.

Panicky, Cara looked for the lifeguard, but he sat high on his lifeguard stand and was too far away. That left one thing to do. She tore off her shorts and Tee, then ran across the hot sand for the ocean, feeling nearly naked in the red bikini.

"Ah-ooo! Oooh, baby!" the guys yelled at her.

"Didn't I tell you guys?" Rolf shouted after her. "She's one v-e-r-y c-u-t-e ba-bee!"

She splashed into the cool surf, trying to find Jess, Tricia, and Becky farther out in the water. Finally, she spotted them and waved. "Hey, here I come!" she yelled over the roar of the ocean. "Wait for me!"

They didn't hear, but she kept moving along. The waves rose higher and higher, breaking and slamming against her as they rushed toward the beach.

When she glanced back, she was glad to see that Rolf and his friends had moved back to where they'd first settled. Bear had returned to their place now, probably to stand guard over the food and drinks. It looked like maybe Bear had told the guys to stay away.

Finally, she caught up with Jess, Tricia, and Becky, but she was deep enough in the water so they'd only see her shoulders.

"Here comes Cara!" Jess yelled before a huge wave raced at her. She dove into it at just the right moment, then went skimming along as a good bodysurfer should.

Tricia bounced along, treading water. Her reddish-blond hair streamed down her back, and her green eyes sparkled as she looked around. "The waves are great! Wouldn't it be perfect to have a boogie board!"

Becky pushed her wet dark hair away from her face. She was the closest to Cara, and her blue eyes opened wide. "Whoa, you wore a bikini—"

Cara pretended not to hear and dove into the next wave. Her hair would be sopping like theirs, but it didn't matter. Anything to forget her growing troubles, and riding along with a wave helped a lot. When the wave slowed near the shore, she glanced at the guys on the beach, but they seemed to have forgotten about her.

She headed back for the deep water near her friends, then dove into another wave, then another. Sometimes the waves somersaulted her through the salty water, even scraped her knees against the sea's rough bottom, but it didn't matter. Out in the ocean, it seemed that time no longer existed, and she'd never have to face her troubles again.

After what seemed hours, Jess and the others yelled, "Come on in, Cara. Bear says we've been out long enough."

She caught another wave and bodysurfed toward shore. How could she get to her beach towel without making a big show of her skimpy red and white bikini?

When she got to her feet to walk the rest of the way in, she was amazed to find Rolf waiting on shore for her with a beach towel—*her* beach towel, at that!

"Hey, ba-bee," he said, "I figured you'd want this."

"Thanks!" She grabbed it and wrapped it round and round herself. "How'd you know?"

His brown eyes seemed to bore right into hers. "I heard it's a Sunday school party, and I figured you're an outsider. You know, seein' you wearin' that bikini."

Cara felt heat pour into her cheeks, but she just pushed back her wet hair. "Thanks again."

They walked along the beach together a little way. "By the way, my name's Rolf Ramesh." He kicked up a spray of dry sand. "What's yours?"

It'd be safe to tell her first name, she decided. "Cara. Just Cara."

"Cara," he repeated. "That's a nice name." Rolf's eyes had a wolfish gleam in them, and he smelled peculiar. "Think you'd go out with me, Cara?"

She felt half-scared and half-thrilled, but she shook her head. "No, thanks anyhow." A second later, she was glad she'd refused because it was beer she smelled on him, even here with the ocean breeze. Had he been drinking the whole time she'd been swimming? And, now that she saw him up close, he looked like he was almost twenty years old.

"I don't give up easy," Rolf added. "Besides, your friends there, they don't like what you wore."

"What do you mean?"

He shrugged a little. "I heard 'em. They say you were supposed to wear *modest* swimsuits. *M-o-d-e-s-t*. Me, I like your little bikini."

Cara glanced at the kids in the Sunday school group. They were watching her and Rolf with interest. All of them except Jess, Tricia, and Becky, who looked on with bare-faced disapproval.

"Remember, I don't give up easy," Rolf said again as he walked away in the sand. He winked and flashed her another handsome smile. "Not me, Cara ba-bee."

Suddenly, Cara wished that Paige had never ever bought this dumb bikini.

CHAPTER

10

"W hat did he want?" Jess asked as Cara settled beside them, still wrapped in her beach towel.

"Nothing much," Cara answered, deciding it wasn't quite a lie. They'd have a fit if they knew he'd asked her for a date. "He said, though, that you'd been talking about me not wearing a *m-o-d-e-s-t* swimsuit."

"That *is* what they told us to wear," Tricia answered. "Bikinis give guys . . . you know, ideas. We're at a junior high Sunday school party at our neighborhood beach, not at some wild party—"

"Never mind! And don't start that again about dancing at the devil's doorstep!" Cara snapped and turned away.

Most of the kids were lined up at the picnic table and helping themselves to hot dogs, corn, and chips. "I'm hungry. Would I be allowed to eat?"

"I'm ready," Jess announced, as if she hadn't even heard the discussion.

"Come on," Tricia said. "Those hot dogs smell good." She didn't look at Cara, though, as she tugged down the bottom of her own modest bathing suit.

Cara glanced at Rolf and the other older guys as she stood up. They were still there, and Rolf was watching. He smiled at her, but she pretended to be looking past him, far along the coastline. She felt angry and spiteful and she-didn't-know-what-else. On top of her money being stolen and her troubles with Paige, now she had to suffer through her friends' very obvious disapproval.

To spite them, she dropped the beach towel to show off her bikini and marched over to the picnic table, where she helped herself to two hot dogs and lots of mustard and pickle relish. If Tricia and Becky and these Sunday school kids didn't like the way she looked, that was their problem.

Finally, they returned to their beach towels to eat. She guessed the bikini was why none of her so-called friends had much to say. Well, phooey on them. Every time she glanced over at Rolf, she saw that he was watching her.

It wasn't until they finished eating that she put on her shorts and yellow polka-dotted shirt. She raked her damp hair back with her fingers. "Come on, let's go home."

"Already?" Tricia asked. "There'll be more volleyball and other games."

"Let's go!" Cara yelled.

"What's wrong with you?" Jess asked. "You're okay now that your bathing suit is covered up."

"Oh, shut up!" Cara answered. "Shut up, all of you!"

Their eyes looked like they'd pop out of their sockets, but they put on their shorts and tops without arguing.

As they pedaled their bikes up the bike lane on Ocean

Avenue, Cara grew even madder. It was bad enough that Paige was awful, that Mom didn't act like she loved her, and that her hard-earned money was stolen—but now her friends objected to her wearing a bikini when she couldn't help it! Maybe she should have explained to them, but at the moment she sure didn't feel like explaining anything.

For a change, she rode the lead bike, and she pedaled as fast as she could, clenching her jaw hard.

"Hey, Cara ba-bee!" someone yelled from a white pickup truck in the next lane.

She glanced over.

Rolf!

He waved from the driver's seat of the pickup, and she returned a grim smile.

"Meet me at the Seven-Eleven on the next corner," he yelled. "Something important to tell you."

"I can't!" she answered.

"Who's stopping you?" he shouted and drove on.

Up ahead, she saw him make a right turn up the steep driveway to the Seven-Eleven convenience store.

Behind her, Tricia yelled, "Cara, you're not going to do it! Those guys must be twenty years old!"

"Oh, can't I!" Cara shouted back. She was tired of acting like a scared doormat. "And don't you dare follow me, any of you! Leave me alone!"

Pedaling hard, she pulled up the steep driveway herself and yelled back another, "Leave me alone!"

They looked appalled as they rode their bikes on around the corner, but she didn't care.

She pedaled to the top of the short hill where the Seven-Eleven stood in a small shopping center. Rolf had already parked his pickup truck right in front, and his two friends climbed out and headed into the store.

"Hey, Cara ba-bee," he said as she coasted her bike to a stop beside his window. "Glad you listened. I was watching you at the beach, and, you know, I really like you. I liked the way you flung yourself into those waves, and the way you paraded around in that little bikini."

She blushed, but her face felt sunburned, so it probably didn't show.

"I thought we should get to know each other better," he said. "You know, go out."

She blurted, "My dad won't let me date."

"Who mentioned a date?" Rolf asked, grinning and looking even more handsome. "I thought we could go for a ride and talk. You know, just get to know each other."

Maybe that wasn't quite a date, Cara decided, not sure. Anyhow, he'd been nice to bring her the beach towel . . . and she was still mad enough to do whatever she pleased. "Okay. What time?"

He smiled and glanced at his watch. "Ummm . . . how about seven-thirty? We could meet right here."

She had the strangest feeling, like someone was watching them. She glanced up and, for a crazy instant, thought she saw Jess behind one of the Seven-Eleven's orange garbage cans. It *had* to be her imagination! Even Jess wouldn't do such a crazy thing!

"Seven-thirty right here," Rolf repeated.

She lifted her chin to prove she wasn't scared. "I'll be here."

As soon as Cara walked in the door of her house the phone rang, and she picked it up. It was Jess.

"Cara, I heard what that guy said to you," Jess admitted. "I came back and listened."

"So?"

"Cara, you can't meet him tonight. It could lead to all kinds of trouble. For all you know, he might be the kidnapper who's been on the TV news."

"You're crazy!"

"Besides, your parents say you aren't old enough to date."

"Mind your own business!" Cara snapped.

"Tricia and Becky said I should beg you for them, too," Jess got in.

"Tell them to mind their own business, too!" she yelled and hung up the phone. Why couldn't they just leave her alone? If she wanted to ruin her life, that was her business, and they should just stay out!

The phone began to ring again, but she didn't answer it.

At seven-thirty, Cara walked across Ocean Avenue to the Seven-Eleven. Her newly washed hair bounced around the shoulders of her white Tee, and she wiped her damp palms on her jeans. No one had been home because Paige was out, so it'd been easy to eat a TV-dinner, put on Mom's lipstick, and leave a note saying, *I'll be with my friends.* Her parents would think it meant Jess, Tricia, and Becky. Maybe it was lying, but it was done.

As she reached the other side of Ocean Avenue, memories flashed to mind: Bear reading "Honor your father and mother, as the Lord your God has commanded you . . ." And her father's firm "No dates." Next came Tricia's "dancing on the devil's doorstep," and the talk about evil.

No! Cara thought, fighting a sudden surge of fear. *I'll do what I want to do! And I'll show Paige that I don't have to grab a guy out of a pool to get his attention. Besides, it's too late now!*

She was about to start up the driveway to the Seven-Eleven when Rolf pulled up beside her in a beat-up green van. Her heart began to pound and she thought fleetingly of making a run for it, but Rolf called out, "Come here, Cara ba-bee."

As she approached the van, she saw that his friends were with him. Fear dried her throat. "I—I thought we'd be alone."

Rolf winked at her. "We will be."

Panic overtook her. "I—I've . . . changed my mind."

"Ain't no time to change your mind, Cara ba-bee," Rolf said soothingly and climbed out of the van. "Come on. We'll have a good time." He reached for her hand.

"N—no," she protested.

He grabbed her hands and pulled her toward the van. "Get in!" he barked. "And don't give us any trouble."

"You're hurting me!" she cried, then realized he meant to. In his narrowed eyes, she saw for the first time what she knew to be evil. "Help!" she shouted, trying to pull away. "H-e-l-p!"

"Run, Cara!" a familiar voice shouted from behind the closest orange garbage can, and Jess popped up.

"Run!" Becky and Tricia shouted and popped up from behind two more garbage cans. "Don't go with him!"

"Help!" she yelled again, for he wouldn't let go.

PLOP! PLOP! PLOP!

Three water balloons whizzed through the air and landed—splat—right on Rolf's head, arms, and chest.

"Run, Cara, run!" her friends shouted again as another barrage of brightly colored water balloons came zinging through the air down to the van.

Astounded and sopping wet, Rolf loosened his grip and Cara tore away. She raced around the corner while three orange garbage cans rolled downhill toward the van.

Up by the store, someone shouted, "Call the security cop!"

Reaching her friends, Cara turned in time to see Rolf backing the van frantically, then roaring it out onto Ocean Avenue.

"Good riddance!" Jess shouted after them fiercely, and Cara started shaking all over. "Good riddance!" Jess yelled again.

Cara was still wet and shaking when Tricia grabbed her and held her tight. "We were so worried about you, and with everyone's parents gone, we did what seemed right. Oh, Cara, forgive us if we were wrong."

For a moment, Cara just rested in her friend's arms, feeling safe and secure . . . and loved.

Finally she stopped shaking and stepped back. "I'm the one who was asking for trouble. I really was dancing on the devil's doorstep. If you hadn't been here throwing water balloons and rolling those crazy garbage cans, I'm afraid to think of . . . what might have happened."

"We knew we had to come," Tricia said, and the others nodded in absolute agreement.

Suddenly Paige's red Thunderbird screeched into the parking lot. She flung her door open and jumped out. "Are you . . . are you okay, Cara?"

Cara stood there in shock. "How'd you know something was wrong?"

"Jess's message on my answering machine . . . something about my b-blasted bikini," Paige sputtered, "and you going out with older guys. Lots older. All I could think about was that kidnapper in the news—"

"I didn't go. My . . . my friends came just in time so I couldn't be forced into their van—"

Paige blew out a grateful breath. "Thank goodness! Thank goodness, you're safe. Come on, I'll drive you home."

Cara turned to her friends, and for the first time, she truly understood how God could use people, how He might send them when you were in trouble. They'd known to come after her, just like she'd known to rescue Brad Tucker in the pool.

"Go on," Jess told her. "We'll clean up the garbage cans. Let your sister take you home now."

They didn't have to say the other words because Cara saw what they meant on their faces: They were truly her friends. They loved her. They loved her a humongous lot.

"Thanks," she told them. "Thanks for everything."

They all nodded, so she got into Paige's car. As she buckled up, it occurred to her how different Becky's and Tricia's families were. They weren't perfect, but they usually got along a whole lot better than hers. Even Jess's was changing for the better since her dad had rededicated himself to God.

Paige put the car into gear, and they roared through the parking lot. They had to wait to pull onto Ocean Avenue, though, and Paige didn't say a word. The car's motor idling filled the silence.

Finally, Cara said, "I decided myself to wear your old bikini, Paige. That was my own mistake. But I *know* you stole my money. I *know* it. And I know you planted that R movie for us to watch, just like you tripped me at the Tuckers' party. You hate me! You want to ruin my life!"

"I don't hate you, I don't!" Paige protested. She let out a deep breath and backed up the car a few feet, then pulled over to the side of the road. Turning the engine off she faced Cara.

"It's just that . . . I ran out of money and owed someone."

Cara was surprised to see Paige truly looking sorry.

"I'll pay you, I promise," Paige said. "I'll pay you back. I'll work at Flicks or somewhere else."

"But why do you hate me, Paige? I really don't understand what I ever did . . ."

Paige pounded a hand on the steering wheel. "Maybe it's because you have a real father . . . one who didn't run off when you were a baby. It makes me so mad sometimes that . . . that I just want to hurt everyone!"

Cara stared at her. *Paige was mean because her heart hurt, because she hurt a lot.* It was the last thing she'd expected.

"I'm sorry," Cara said, "really sorry."

"It's not your fault."

"I guess not."

They sat in silence again, then Cara said, "Remember how sweet we both were at dinner last night? I guess you were so nice because you'd just taken my money. But why can't we really be nice like that? Why can't we try to be friends and have a good family?"

Paige pressed her lips together. At last, she said, "I'll try from now on. I'll really try!" She looked hard at Cara for an instant. "Does that mean you forgive me?"

"Forgive you?" Cara asked.

Paige nodded.

Forgive Paige?

She remembered Tricia and Becky forgiving her for showing the R movie because Christians were supposed to forgive. She remembered Bear reading the Ten Commandments that God had given to help everyone. *LOOK TO GOD FOR ALL THE ANSWERS*, his T-shirt at the beach had said.

In her heart, it seemed that God was saying He loved her, that He'd shown His love through her friends coming to her rescue. Quite suddenly, she felt an overwhelming surge of love.

"I will," she said, "only I'll have to learn how to do it . . . you know, how to forgive. Guess I'll have to forgive that Rolf, too, whether or not we ever know if he was a kidnapper."

Even before speaking the next words, she knew they were true. They came to her lips with awe and wonder. "I'm going to learn how to forgive because . . . I'm going to become a Christian."

"You are?" Paige asked, amazed.

"I am," Cara answered. She recalled Tricia's prayer—that God would use the missing money in a miraculous way. He had done it, because Cara knew that she was in the midst of a miracle. She announced it again with a burst of joyous excitement. "I really am going to become a Christian."

"Why? Why would you do that?"

There were lots of reasons to sort out, but Cara knew one for sure: It had to do with her special friends in the Twelve Candles Club. "I guess it's partly because my friends showed how much they love me, even if it was embarrassing to do."

"You know," Paige said as if she began to understand, "I almost wish I had friends like that."

She gave a little laugh at the idea of it, and Cara had to laugh herself since she couldn't imagine Paige in such a situation. Suddenly they were laughing more and more, then harder and harder.

For the first time Cara could remember, they were laughing together. In the midst of it she gasped, "You mean wacko friends who'd roll garbage cans down to save you?"

"Yeah," Paige answered. "Wacko friends like that!"